Sure Shot in Las Capas: The Case of the Absent Star

(A Cobalt City Universe Story)

Dawn Vogel

Cover Art by Luke Spooner

DEDICATION

To Nathan Crowder, who always said "yes" when I asked if I could
make another member of the Huntsman legacy

Other Cobalt City Universe Stories

By Nathan Crowder
Greetings From Buena Rosa (2006, Timid Pirate Publishing)
Ride Like the Devil (2007, Timid Pirate Publishing; reprinted 2018, DefCon One Publishing)
Chanson Noir: Protectorate Vol. 1 (2009, Timid Pirate Publishing)
Cobalt City Blues: Protectorate Vol. 2 (2010, Timid Pirate Publishing)
Cobalt City: Los Muertos (2014)
Cobalt City: Ties that Bind (2015; reprinted 2018, DefCon One Publishing)
Cobalt City: Resistance (2018)

By Amanda Cherry
Rites and Desires (2018, Def Con One Publishing)

By Erik Scott de Bie
Eye for an Eye (originally published as a part of *Cobalt City Double Feature*, 2012, Timid Pirate Publishing; reprinted 2018, DefCon One Publishing)

By Dawn Vogel
Sparx and Arrows (2016, DefCon One Publishing)
Coast to Coast Stars (2020, DefCon One Publishing)

By Jeremy Zimmerman
Kensei (originally published as a part of *Cobalt City Rookies*, 2012, Timid Pirate Publishing; reprinted 2014, DefCon One Publishing)
The Love of Danger (2015, DefCon One Publishing)
The Devil, You Say (2015, DefCon One Publishing)
Snowflake War Journal (2016, DefCon One Publishing)
Kensei Tales: Offensive Driving (2016, DefCon One Publishing)
Kensei Tales: It's the Great Yule Cat, Jamie Hattori (2016, DefCon One Publishing)
Kensei Tales: Live and In Concert (2017, DefCon One Publishing)
Kensei Tales: Unorthodoxy (2017, Def Con One Publishing)

Cobalt City Anthologies
Cobalt City Christmas (2009, Timid Pirate Publishing)
Cobalt City Timeslip (2010, Timid Pirate Publishing)
Cobalt City Dark Carnival (2011, Timid Pirate Publishing)
Cobalt City Double Feature (2012, Timid Pirate Publishing, featuring *Eye for an Eye* by Erik Scott de Bie and *The Place Between* by Minerva Zimmerman)
Cobalt City Rookies (2012, Timid Pirate Publishing, featuring *Tatterdemalion* by Nikki Burns, *Wrecker of Engines* by Rosemary Jones, and *Kensei* by Jeremy Zimmerman)
Cobalt City Christmas: Christmas Harder (2016)

CONTENTS

CHAPTER ONE

When you're washing the dinner dishes, you're not expecting an explosion. Unless you're me, in which case you're more surprised to discover said explosion wasn't directed at you.

The blast was enough to rattle the window above the kitchen sink. My training kicked in, and I dropped to a crouch, certain I was about to have glass raining down on my back. I counted under my breath, like you might with the time between lightning and thunder, or in between the tremors of an earthquake and its aftershocks.

I only got to five before Daisy called out to me from the living room. "Sarah? Are you alright?"

I took a quick stock of my situation. I seemed to be all in one piece, though my apron was soaked, the dampness penetrating through to my dress and nylons. I'd gotten out of what I thought of as the line of fire, but I'd been careful to cradle the plate I was washing, to make sure it didn't slip from my grip onto the floor. I suddenly felt foolish. "I'm fine," I called back.

But Daisy was already in the doorway, her head cocked to the side as she looked at my wet apron and the plate. "That's my girl," she chuckled, though her eyes were still serious. "Really, though, are you okay?"

I took a deep breath. The Western Front of the Second World War was far away—farther now that I was living in California instead of D.C.—but there had been enough nights that I'd woken on the verge of a scream, tangled in our bed sheets, that Daisy knew how often the War haunted my dreams. She was always able to soothe me back to sleep, and I was sure she was pondering how to calm me now. Setting the plate in the sink carefully, I dried my hands and untied my apron. "I'm alright, but maybe I should finish the dishes later."

"I'll take care of the dishes, Sarah."

"Nonsense. You cooked, I'll clean. It's only fair." It was the way of our relationship—we shared the chores, rather than either of us becoming the "housewife."

"If you insist." But her gaze flickered pointedly toward my small home office. "Go make some calls and find out what happened. You'll feel better knowing."

A whine like a small propeller plane passed over the house, drawing my attention to the ceiling. For me, at least, the sound was unmistakable. "That's General Justice, heading toward the bay."

I followed Daisy back into the living room, where she'd been reading through scripts sent over by her agent. Having worked her way up from small acting jobs, now she was getting to choose which projects she took. She left the scripts strewn about and drew back the living room curtains, revealing a fire in the middle of Las Capas Bay.

The trailing light of General Justice's rocket boots was far enough from our house that it did little to illuminate the water, but the implication of an explosion followed by a fire in the bay was that a boat had been the target. General Justice being first on the scene was no surprise, either—Retired Air Forces General Richard Justice was known as the preeminent superhero of Las Capas, and his house wasn't too far from ours, just a bit farther up the hillside for a more commanding view of the bay.

"Well, if General Justice is on the case, I guess there's not much for you to do," Daisy said gently. Though I was retired from the superhero life, it hadn't been all that long ago that I had been actively fighting crime. It stung a little to be left out, and Daisy did her best to not reopen that wound.

But she was right. I didn't fly or swim, so my helpfulness at a crime scene in the middle of the bay would be non-existent. At best, I might get called in to help with the investigation, if this wasn't an open and closed case.

"Only one boat out there tonight," I mused, the wheels in my head already turning over the details I had.

"Seems like there should have been more?" Daisy asked. She loved playing along with my investigations, whether we were speculating about the secret lives of our neighbors or it was a case I'd been hired to work.

"It looked like a storm earlier, so perhaps not." I tried to estimate the size of the boat based on General Justice's silhouetted form. "It's not a fishing boat. Something a little larger, but not ostentatious." I wasn't likely to spot the name painted on the side of the boat, but I craned my neck all the same.

A jagged streak of icy blue arced across the sky, coming to a quick stop just above the fiery wreckage, and a moment later, the flames began to subside, as Ciclón opened a small rainstorm on the boat. She'd moved quickly to arrive here from the east side of the city. Or perhaps she'd been out on patrol and spotted the explosion from her vantage point in the skies.

"Front row seats to some superheroics," Daisy said. "Remind you of home?"

I shrugged. It did, even if Cobalt City had dramatically greater numbers of superheroes than Las Capas, or even the whole of Cerulean City. But I'd left Cobalt City and the disapproving gaze of my father, and I'd left the mantle of the Huntsman to my brother, Matthew—entirely, now, unlike during the War, when we both wore the cape and cowl, he in the States and me in Europe.

Nights like this reminded me why. In spite of our family legacy of protecting Cobalt City, the Huntsman had never had powers—just skill. General Justice had his self-built power suit, and Ciclón had inborn powers. They were the heavy hitters. Other superheroes, some powered and some not, filled the second string. I would come in as third string, at best, if I were still doing the superhero thing.

Which I wasn't, I reminded myself, letting my half of the curtains drop back into place. If my services were needed in this case as an investigator, my answering service would let me know.

"I think the show's over for now, Daisy. Do you want any help practicing your lines?"

Daisy released the other side of the curtains and looked at me wistfully. "No, I'll help you finish the dishes, and then I think we could both use an early night tonight. My makeup call is early, and you may have a case."

"How do you figure?"

"A boat that size could belong to half of the *nouveau riche* in Las Capas. Someone's going to want to know why it exploded." She grimaced. "And who was on it."

~

The next morning, I picked up the newspaper from the front porch. My eyes were bleary until I had my coffee, so dropped the paper on the table and busied myself with getting out dishes, awaiting the coffee Daisy was brewing. Only Daisy's sudden gasp pulled me out of my morning routine.

She stood with the coffee pot in one hand, her other hand over her mouth, and a look of shock in her eyes.

"What's wrong, did you burn yourself?" I asked.

She shook her head and pointed to the paper.

The headline read: "Warren Glenn Victim of Boat Explosion."

My heart plummeted into my stomach. Warren Glenn was one of the leading men of Las Capas, starring in half a dozen pictures each year. But I knew him as Invincible Man, an identity he worked hard to hide from his adoring fans. And though some superheroes exaggerated their powers when naming themselves, Warren hadn't, or so I believed. He was supposed to be truly invincible and had proven incredible physical resilience on numerous occasions. But if the newspaper headline was true, someone had found a way around his powers.

Daisy set down the coffee pot with a shaky hand. "He's the lead in the film I'm working on right now."

I regained enough of my senses to wrap an arm around her shoulders. Though she and I had lived together as a couple for the better part of two years, the secrets of a certain subset of my associates hadn't reached her ears. I was busy trying to puzzle out what happened. She was grieving a co-worker. "Sit. Let me finish making breakfast."

With a mute nod, she sat, her gaze sweeping across the article below the headline. "He's been ... there have been a couple of times when he's invited some of the other cast to go out on his boat. He might not be the only victim."

I poured her coffee slowly, not wanting my own hands to reveal how shaken I was. "Does it say anything about others?"

She shook her head, then began reading as I turned back to the stove to salvage what I could of the eggs she was frying. "'Police and citizens who arrived on the scene could not confirm the boat's passengers at this time, but the police have stated a strong likelihood that Glenn's body will be identified before long. It remains to be seen if other victims are also identified.' It says his driver is unaccounted for, but it looks like that's all so far."

Toast popped out of the toaster, and I hurried it onto our plates, then topped each of them with a fried egg, a little more cooked than either of us liked them. Sitting beside Daisy, I poured my own coffee, then slid the paper closer as I took my first sip.

She'd read the gist of the interesting parts, as the majority of the article seemed to be more of an obituary for Warren Glenn, even as it acknowledged that perhaps he hadn't been on his own boat. Reading between the lines, I half wondered if the reporter was in on Warren's secret identity as a superhero—her use of "two concerned citizens" where some reporters might have identified General Justice and Ciclón was telling.

With a few bites of her breakfast eaten, Daisy gave me a wan smile. "Are you heading to your office today?"

"I don't know yet. I'll check in with Catherine after breakfast," I said, still perusing the newspaper. "I'm curious about this, but I don't know if there's a case, or whether it will come my way. They haven't ruled out mechanical malfunction as a cause of the explosion." Even as I said the words, I suspected General Justice might already know if mechanical malfunction was likely or not, but he'd give any charred remains of the boat a thorough examination before making a statement speaking to that. I could find out if I gave him a call.

"Do you think you've got time to drive me to the studio, then? I'm not sure I'm in any state to be behind the wheel this morning."

I nodded. "I certainly do, and I'll even pick you up this evening too."

Daisy smiled. She wasn't often taken to play the damsel in distress, but she depended on me for my logical coolness and stability now and then.

"What time do you suppose you'll be done?" I asked.

"Well, the schedule said six tonight, but things may have changed." She sighed. "Sarah, I just can't believe it. Warren Glenn has asked *me* to go out on his boat. I could have been there with him!"

"But you weren't," I assured her. "And you've never been on the boat, have you?"

She shook her head. "No, he's not my type."

I chuckled at that understatement—though both Daisy and I had gone on dates with men in the past, we had never had steady relationships before finding one another—then shrugged. "The truth is there are all sorts of things that could take us out of this world at any moment. Heaven knows I've seen more than my fair share. But we're both still here."

Daisy smiled, her eyes lighting up with real joy as she leaned in to give me a quick kiss. "And I'm all the happier for that." Her gaze slid up to the clock. "But if I'm going to make my make-up call, I'd better shake a leg."

~

Daisy had people to do her make-up when she got to work. I had to do my own, simple though it was, which meant we were still home when the phone rang.

"Sarah, it's Catherine," Daisy called.

Catherine was my secretary, more or less. I didn't have enough clients to maintain a nine to five office presence, so I'd hired her as an answering service—she took appointments via phone and let me know when I needed to be at the office. She did similar work for other PIs and half a dozen other professionals in the Las Capas area.

Picking up the phone receiver from where Daisy had left it, I said, "Morning, Catherine. Got something for me today?"

"Morning to you too, Sarah. And yes, got a call for you first thing this morning. A little overly distraught, but I got the details worked out. She agreed to a one p.m., but if you can do earlier, she'd take that."

I wasn't surprised to hear the potential client was a woman. Something about a female PI seemed to ease the minds of other women. In Las Capas, it meant she suspected her husband was cheating on her, which meant weeks of late nights at seedy bars. It wasn't my favorite work, but it paid the bills.

I glanced at the clock and did some calculating. "I've got a bit of running around to do this morning, so let's keep it at one. What's the case?"

"Oh, you'll like this one, I think. It's a double case. Investigating a murder and a missing person."

That was a bit of a twist. "Does she think they're related?"

Catherine chuckled. "In a manner of speaking, yes. The prospective client is one Clarisse Glenn."

My eyebrows raised at that. "Clarisse Glenn, as in—"

"Sister of Warren Glenn, yes. She wants you to find out who killed Warren, because she's certain it was murder, but also find out where her other brother, Archibald, might have gotten off to."

Daisy had come back into the living room, and I looked in her direction, my expression still one of surprise. She returned my gaze, but with a more quizzical quirk to her eyebrows. Lurking behind that, though, I could still see her nerves weren't all they should be today. I'd promised her a ride to the studio, and I wasn't going to change my plans, no matter how curious I was to meet Warren Glenn's sister and get information on this case.

"Thanks, Catherine. I'll be in the office by one."

"Wonderful, I'll confirm with Miss Glenn."

As I hung up, Daisy asked, "You've got a case?"

My gaze flickered toward the living room windows, curtains drawn back to reveal the bay in all its sun-dappled morning glory. It was a much different sight without the flaming wreckage of a boat in its midst. "You were right. Warren Glenn's sister is coming by my office this afternoon. Not only does she believe Warren might have been murdered, there's a missing brother too."

"Missing, huh? That sounds suspicious."

"Maybe. I'll wait and see what the sister's got."

"Too late, I can see the wheels are already turning in your mind," Daisy said, smiling. "You'll have to give me all the details later."

CHAPTER TWO

———

I made it to my office a little before one and was relieved Clarisse Glenn wasn't waiting. My office wasn't much nicer than the hallway, but at least it had comfortable chairs.

I'd installed heavy blinds in my office to keep the worst of the California heat out. I'd only been here two years, and I hadn't quite acclimated to it. Cobalt City and D.C. both had their fair share of muggy, sweltering summer weather. Las Capas seemed to revel in it year-round, except for those rare days when the ocean breeze blew in from the bay and made everything a lot more pleasant.

Today wasn't one of those days.

A knock on the door heralded Clarisse Glenn's arrival, right as the clock struck one.

"Come in!"

Though I thought of it as an excessively hot day for mid-April, Clarisse Glenn wore a long tan jacket, the sort that passed as a raincoat in this climate. Her dress beneath it was tidy and simple, a pale blue that matched her hat, handbag, and heels, as well as her eyes, the same crystalline blue as Warren Glenn's. But while his hair was on the darker side of brown, hers was a glamourous blonde, curling softly just above her shoulders. The family resemblance was apparent despite their different hair colors.

"You're Miss Castile?" she asked, her accent the broad, indefinable lilt of the Midwestern states.

"Yes, ma'am, and you must be Miss Glenn."

She nodded, closing the door behind her. She removed her jacket but left her hat in place and approached my desk with a gloved hand outstretched. "Please, call me Clarisse."

I shook her hand and smiled. "Thank you, and do call me Sarah. Now, my secretary gave me brief details on your case, but please, have a seat and elaborate."

We each took our respective seats, though Clarisse looked around my office before turning her attention to me. "I seem to have lost both of my brothers in the space of less than a week."

"My condolences for—"

She shook her head. "Please, I realize I told your secretary my brother was murdered. I don't think the explosion was an accident. But until there's a positively identified body, I'm not ready for condolences."

"That's a reasonable approach to take." *Especially for the purported death of Invincible Man.* I couldn't be sure if Warren's secret was one he had shared with his family, though, so I phrased my next question carefully. "But my secretary indicated you want me to investigate the explosion."

"Yes, of course," Clarisse said. "I was told this was the sort of work you've taken on in the past."

I cocked my head to the side. "May I ask who recommended me?"

"Detective Cooper, at the First Precinct."

Detective Jimmy Cooper was with the Las Capas Police Department. Since I'd arrived in Las Capas, I'd made some good connections with the police department—not all cops wanted to work hand in hand with private investigators, but I'd leveraged my war experience into friendships with some officers and detectives who were also veterans. Jimmy also knew I had spent time donning a cape and cowl in Europe, helping the people there when faced with villainy of all sorts. That he'd sent Clarisse to me told me he thought there was a case here, even if his department might not agree.

I nodded. "Detective Cooper has a good eye for making the right connections. Is there anything you can tell me about your brother's boat, or the explosion, anything the general public might not know yet?"

"I don't think so," Clarisse said, shaking her head and peering at the edge of the curtains, where the sunlight peeked through in a narrow sliver. "I don't know a lot about boats, I'm afraid, and Warren hadn't taken us out on it yet."

"Us. You mean you and your other brother, then?"

"Archie. Archibald." She shook her head, gaze directed toward the ceiling, and an exasperated twist to her lips. "He and I came out to visit Warren last week, with plans to stay for a couple of weeks. Archie never came back to our hotel on Saturday night. I've contacted the police, but they seem to think he's just gone back home."

"And you don't think that's the case?"

"I've called his apartment, and he hasn't answered. I haven't quite reached the point of calling his neighbors to ask if they've seen him at home or not."

I picked up a pen and began to take notes. "Where is home for the two of you?"

"Denver. Warren bought train tickets for us to come out. One way, with plans to buy us the return trip when we'd had enough of the California sun. The stationmaster can't tell me if Archie bought a new ticket and left, because he says he sees hundreds of people a day. But he left behind all his clothes. And he wouldn't just up and leave."

"Alright, let's walk through this whole trip, if you don't mind. When did you arrive in Las Capas?"

"Last Wednesday, the thirteenth. We arrived in the evening, and Warren sent a car to take us to the hotel. We didn't see him until Thursday, and he took us on set with him on Friday."

I noted the visit to the set and underlined it. Daisy had been on set on Friday, too, so maybe she'd have seen Clarisse or the mystery brother, Archie. "And then over the weekend?" I prompted Clarisse.

"The last time I saw Archie was Saturday afternoon, after we had lunch with Warren." She shrugged. "I didn't get worried at first, because Archie likes to go out to nightclubs and such, and I thought maybe he'd just stayed out all night. But when he wasn't back by Sunday evening, I started to wonder if maybe he'd gotten into some kind of trouble. That's when I went to the police."

I paused in my notetaking. "If you don't mind my asking, what sort of trouble might he have gotten in?"

Clarisse sighed, her gaze again upward. "He's a bit of a drinker, and his judgment isn't always the best. I thought he could have gotten himself into the drunk tank or something, but the police said they didn't have any record of him being brought in."

"Any chance he might have given a false name?"

Shaking her head vigorously enough that I worried for the safety of her hat, Clarisse said, "Oh, no. Well, at least, I don't think so. Is that ... is that something people do in Las Capas?"

"People have been giving other people false names all across the world for centuries," I said, chuckling softly. "But I'll take your word that it's unlikely he would have done such a thing, and we'll assume he's not drying out in a drunk tank somewhere under an alias. Any other trouble you can think of?"

"I don't know, maybe somebody who wanted to get to Warren."

That gave me pause. There was no socially acceptable way to gently dig into whether someone was known to be a superhero, even amongst members of their immediate family. So I had to continue to ask the standard questions and not let on that I knew anything special about Warren Glenn, at least not until Clarisse gave me any reason to pursue a different line of questioning. "Somebody like?"

With a shrug, she said, "He's got some enemies, I guess. The boys don't tell me what's going on, being their baby sister and all, but I'm sure it's the mob or something."

I frowned at that detail. "What information have you picked up from them that makes you think it's the mob?"

She shrugged again and looked away. "Warren and Archie were whispering about photos and money and blackmail at one point." She returned her gaze to me. "I'm sorry, I guess I don't have a whole lot for you to go on, but I just don't think the police are going to help me find Archie."

I wasn't sure what to make of Clarisse's lack of eye contact with me. It might have been a strange affectation, but it made me suspect she wasn't being entirely honest with me. Still, her recounting was all I had to go on thus far. "Okay, what else can you tell me about Archie? Is he married?"

"Oh, Lord, no," Clarisse said, laughing. "There's not a woman alive who could tie that man down." She hesitated, then clarified. "No man, either. He likes women just fine, just not for anything lasting."

"Do you know anything about the sort of clubs he might have gone to?"

"Anything with good jazz and cheap, strong drinks."

I chuckled softly. "That's not much to go on in Las Capas."

"Usually I see matchbooks he's brought back from the clubs, but Saturday was the first night he went out."

"Do you know if he walked or took a cab?"

"I don't know, sorry."

I glanced over my notes again. "Do you have any more information about Warren and the boat explosion?" Recalling what Daisy had said about Warren Glenn taking other cast members out on his boat, I continued. "Might there have been anyone else with him on the boat?"

Clarisse shook her head. "I don't have any more information about the explosion. All I know is Warren loved his boat, and I assume he took good care of it. The police said they didn't have much more than what the papers were reporting, and their investigation was ongoing." She paused, glancing at me. "Does this mean you'll take the case?"

I nodded. "My secretary gave you my terms, and she said you've already paid for at least two weeks of my time. We're all square in that regard, and I'm willing to investigate the boat explosion and Archie's whereabouts."

"You won't be stepping on the police department's toes by investigating the boat explosion, will you?"

"I'll check in with Detective Cooper to make sure I'm not," I assured her.

"Thank you. When it comes right down to it, I'm more worried about Archie, at this point. Warren could be fine, for all I know. But this isn't like Archie at all."

I nodded, sympathetic. I only had one brother to worry about, though he'd proven quite capable of taking care of himself. Maybe Clarisse realized Warren was similarly competent. And maybe Archie didn't have the same sort of resiliency. "If I need to get in contact with you, how would I do that?"

"We're ... well, I'm, I guess, staying at the Grand." She dug a card out of her handbag. "Let's see here, the number is Las Capas-51218."

I noted the number. "Alright, I'll give you a call if I get any strong leads, or if I have any more questions for you."

"Thank you, Miss ... I mean, Sarah."

~

13

I headed to the First Precinct of the Las Capas Police Department after my meeting with Clarisse and spotted Jimmy Cooper as soon as I walked in, just beyond the front desk. He wasn't particularly tall for a man, barely taller than me when I was wearing heels, but he exuded a strong presence with his ramrod bearing and sharp gray eyes. His hair remained as short as it had been when he was in the Service, dark, without even a hint of silver, though he was a few years my senior.

I waved at him as I signed the visitor's log. "Detective Cooper, good to see you. Do you have a minute?"

He smiled. "For you, I've got ten."

I returned his smile and followed him into his office. His desk was a mess of paperwork and folders, but I knew him well enough to know that if he needed any piece of information, he could pick it out in an instant.

"Glenn case, I'm guessing?" he asked as soon as we'd both sat down.

"Good guess."

"Which part did the sister hire you for?"

"Both."

He sighed. "Officially speaking, we don't think there's much of a case with Archibald. If there's anything there, though, you'll find it for her."

"Thanks for the vote of confidence. Has Warren Glenn's body been recovered?"

He shook his head, his lips a tight line. "Not yet, but they're sending divers down into the bay today. We can't get an official proclamation of death until they recover a body."

I caught his wording. "A body? Not Warren Glenn's body?"

Jimmy gave me a stern look. "Let's just say we don't know what we'll find."

As far as I was aware, Warren hadn't revealed his secret identity to the police force. That didn't mean Jimmy didn't know, though. Detectives were good at ferreting out secrets. I nodded, matching Jimmy's gaze. "Sure, that makes sense. And you don't think there's much to find out about Archibald Glenn?"

"If there's a body found, Archibald Glenn moves from a potentially missing person to a person of interest. Though our best guess is he's already back in Denver."

"Clarisse doesn't seem to think he would have left without her. But he's a suspect?"

"Yeah, Warren and Archie had a bit of a public tiff on Saturday afternoon at Reginald's, over on Fortieth."

The Reginald's he referred to was an upscale restaurant, popular among actors and studio executives. And Clarisse had mentioned lunch with Warren on Saturday, before Archie disappeared. "What was the tiff about?"

"Money is the impression I got from talking to some of the witnesses." He paused, inclining his head. "The sister didn't mention it?"

I shook my head. "She left that bit out."

"Hmm, that's interesting." Leaning back in his chair, he asked, "What was your impression of her?"

"I got the sense she might have been leaving a few things out," I admitted. "Overall, though, I think she's in a bit of shock. As far as she knows, she's just lost one of her brothers, if not both."

"Sure, I guess that would cloud a person's judgment."

I arched my eyebrow. "You think she's got her judgment clouded?"

"Well, she was distraught when she came in to report Archie's disappearance on Sunday night. Much moreso than when we contacted her to inform her of Warren's boat exploding."

I thought about my conversation with Clarisse and nodded. "You're right, she's far more concerned that something untoward has happened to Archie. She hired me to investigate the boat explosion and find Archie, but she spent far more time telling me Archie couldn't have gone back to Denver." I frowned. "Have you considered her as a suspect?"

Jimmy leaned forward. "In the explosion? I suppose it's possible, but she did seem surprised when we gave her the news."

I shook my head, smiling. "Jimmy, we live in a city filled with actors. Surely you've had a woman lie to you before."

"Sure, all the time." He chuckled. "But that wasn't the read I got from her. You?"

"I suppose not. And if I had two brothers, and had killed one and lost the other, I wouldn't hire someone like me to figure out both halves of the problem. Though I suppose, too, it would look suspicious if she'd only hired me to look for the missing brother and not to find out what happened to the dead brother."

"Believed dead," Jimmy corrected me.

I smiled coyly. "About that? Believed?"

"No body, no death certificate."

With a slight tilt of my head, I said, "Jimmy, I'm from Cobalt City."

"And I'm following protocol. But you're a smart lady. I'll let you draw your own conclusions."

"Fair enough," I said, rising from my seat. "I appreciate the ten minutes, Detective Cooper. Thanks for the tip on Reginald's."

He rose as well and opened the door to his office to see me out. "Any time, Miss Castile."

~

I headed straight to Reginald's from my meeting with Jimmy. An argument about money in Las Capas could be anything from who was paying the lunch tab to something related to Archie and Clarisse's trip from Denver and who was paying for which aspects of that. Or maybe even something more substantial. I liked and trusted Jimmy, but I knew some of the other cops in his Precinct would have heard "rich people were arguing about money" and accepted that as the whole story. I suspected there might be something more going on.

It was almost four when I arrived at the restaurant. They weren't open for dinner yet, but there was a young man, in a starched white shirt and neatly pressed black slacks, rearranging the patio furniture. I couldn't be certain if he was part of the waitstaff or kitchen staff, but he looked as likely a witness as anyone else, so I started with him.

I pulled out an old press pass I carried in my bag—people in Las Capas were much more willing to talk to the press than they were to talk to PIs or cops. There was a level of appeal to seeing your name (or "an anonymous witness," when you knew that was you) in print that often loosened lips. And I'd learned some journalism strategies from my father.

I flashed the young man my biggest smile and said, "Hi, I'm Sarah Castile of the *Cobalt Liberty*, could I ask you a couple of questions, Mister, ah—"

He glanced toward the open door of the restaurant. "Uh, sorry, we're not open until five."

"Oh, I understand, I'm not trying to get a table. I'm working on a piece about Mr. Warren Glenn, and I understand he had lunch here on Saturday. Were you working the lunch shift on Saturday?"

He averted his gaze but nodded sharply. "Yeah, I was here."

I flipped out a small notepad. "Can I get your name?"

"Uh, Vic."

"Last name, Vic?"

"Look, I'd rather not get my name in your paper, if it's all the same to you, ma'am."

"Anonymous witness, then. Did you happen to overhear the ... well, let's call it a disagreement between Mr. Glenn and his brother?"

Vic nodded sharply again. "Yeah, you couldn't have been within a block of here and not heard it. They were loud."

"Who you talking to, Vic?" a voice called from inside the restaurant. A woman stepped out and looked me over. She wore similar clothing to Vic, though she had a spotless plain black apron over her blouse and slacks. Her auburn hair was pulled into a fancy looped braid, and she was a decade or two older than Vic. "Oh, a reporter?"

I repeated my introduction to the woman, and added, "Just asking a couple of questions about the rather loud disagreement that happened here Saturday."

She laughed. "Figures someone would come creeping around looking for the gossip. Yeah, one of them had all the money and he wouldn't give it to the other one."

"One of them?" I asked, frowning. "Well, wouldn't it have been Mr. Warren Glenn, the actor, with all the money?"

"Maybe," she shrugged. "They looked just the same though, and they moved around enough I couldn't be sure which one was which."

I flipped a few pages in my notebook to notes from an old case while I digested that. If Warren and Archie looked similar, why had no one else mentioned that? How had the tabloids not picked up on Warren Glenn having a look-alike brother, especially if Archie was the sort to go out to nightclubs. "Sorry, I didn't catch your name?"

"Maggie Lewis. My grandfather is Reginald Lewis. The Reginald of Reginald's."

"A pleasure, Miss Lewis. And may I quote you in my article?"

17

"It'd be best if you didn't," she said, crossing her arms over her chest.

"Of course. Now are you saying Mr. Archibald Glenn and Mr. Warren Glenn looked similar enough that you couldn't tell them apart? Are they twins?"

Miss Lewis nodded. "They could be, yeah. I know Mr. Warren Glenn's an actor, but the other one would have made a fantastic stand-in for the long shots. Even that lady who was with them seemed a little bit confused about what was happening."

I glanced at Vic, who had gone back to arranging the chairs at tables. "Vic, were you able to tell them apart at all?"

"Not really, ma'am. Except one of them got in a car to leave, and the other one walked away, with the woman following him."

"Did you get a sense of what they were arguing about?"

I addressed the question to both of them, but Vic busied himself with the task at hand while Miss Lewis spoke up. "One of them was saying the other one made some bad investments, and they were going to rain down on him like a hail of bullets."

I arched my eyebrow. "That's a rather specific metaphor."

Lowering her voice, she took a step closer to me. "Yeah, that's the one they used. They mentioned the Martinellis and Seacrest Studios." She shrugged. "I wouldn't be spreading that part around too much, though."

Seacrest Studios was the studio for which Warren Glenn had been the leading man—the same one Daisy was contracted to at the moment, though hers was a short-term contract. The Martinellis I knew plenty more about, since their mob ties put them in the crosshairs of every superhero in Las Capas at one time or another. Either of those entities wielded an enormous amount of power in the city. If Warren Glenn was on the outs with either or both, they could be leads on why his boat had been blown up.

I scribbled a few notes in shorthand—I wasn't about to commit the names of either a powerful studio or a mob family to my notes in plain English—and smiled at Miss Lewis and Vic. "Anything else?"

"Something about being replaced. One of them was yelling about the other one being replaceable, maybe?" Miss Lewis's lips twisted and her eyebrows knit as though she was trying to remember more. "I think it was the other brother saying Warren Glenn could be replaced."

"Replaced?" I asked. "Did you get a sense of what Mr. Archibald Glenn might have been referring to?"

Miss Lewis shrugged. "It sounded to me like they were talking about whatever picture Warren Glenn was working on. Or some sort of acting job. But I don't know how true that is. Warren Glenn has a charm like none other."

"He does lead a charmed life," I replied, trying not to smirk. Realizing what I'd said, I clarified. "Or, perhaps he once did. At any rate, thank you both for your assistance. I'll be sure no names are mentioned in the papers."

Granted, this article would never appear either, but I wasn't about to bring that up. I made my way back to my car, puzzling over the newest bits of information. Twins, the mob, the studio, and maybe a rival for Warren's leading man status? Things were getting interesting indeed.

CHAPTER THREE

I didn't have enough time to go back to my office, since I needed to pick up Daisy at six, but I had a couple of phone calls to make, so I popped into a phone booth near Reginald's.

My first call was to Clarisse Glenn, as I needed some answers from her before I could proceed.

"Grand Hotel, how may I direct your call?"

"Sarah Castile, calling for Miss Clarisse Glenn."

"One moment." The clicks of a transferred call followed, and then ringing. I gave it a few rings, not certain what Clarisse's schedule might look like.

Just when I was getting ready to hang up, another set of clicks heralded the return of the operator. "I'm sorry, Miss Castile, it seems perhaps Miss Glenn is out. Would you like to leave a message for her?"

"I don't suppose she gave any indication of when a better time to reach her might be?"

"No, ma'am, I'm afraid she didn't."

"If you don't mind letting her know I called. She has my office number." I considered leaving my home number as well, but I couldn't guarantee anyone would be there to answer it either. At least with my office number, I knew Catherine would answer it if Clarisse called back soon.

"Thank you, ma'am. Have a pleasant day."

Next, I dialed up someone who might have noticed something at the scene of the crime—General Justice.

He answered on the second ring, his voice deep and sonorous. "Justice residence, Richard speaking."

"Hello, Richard. It's Sarah Castile."

"Sarah, good to hear your voice." He paused for the briefest of instants. "What can I help you with?"

"Unpleasant business, I'm afraid. The boat explosion."

"Ah, yes, that is a rather unpleasant matter."

"You haven't heard anything from—" I hesitated, unsure what name to use.

"Our mutual friend?" Richard replied. "No, I haven't. We covered the scene pretty thoroughly, but he didn't appear to be in residence at the time."

I frowned. "Do you think the boat was unpiloted?"

"That's unlikely. But we hoped we might find a survivor or two. No such luck. They're doing a dive today."

"Yes, I talked to the First Precinct earlier."

"Are you working this case now?" Richard asked.

"Yes, and a related case." I gave him the quick version of what Clarisse had hired me for, without too many of the details I'd uncovered so far. We were both busy people, and he'd ask if he needed more information from me. "Do you think they're likely to find anything?"

"Hard to say," he said, with an almost audible shrug. "Between the explosion, the twilight hour, and the bay being a bit more stirred up than usual, my sensors didn't do as well as I'd hoped. I've been fine tuning them, but they're not quite getting the range I'd hoped for."

"Hmm," I said. The technical details were lost on me, so I didn't need a full explanation. "So what you're saying is there may be bodies yet to be found."

"Pretty good odds, I'd say."

"What about the odds that someone survived the explosion?"

He paused briefly before responding. "Longer. But miraculous things happen all the time in Las Capas."

"One more thing—you didn't happen to see anyone out of place keeping an eye on things, did you?"

"Just the usual gawkers, dazzled by the display. My assistant signed more autographs than I did."

"Ouch," I replied, with a teasing note in my voice. "Though I thought your assistant had been upgraded." Ciclón had once been General Justice's sidekick, but they were supposed to have more of an equal partnership these days. Richard, though, had a problem common to many superheroes—he tended to underestimate those who were younger, female, and, in Ciclón's case, not white.

He stammered before he said, "Yes, technically. Of course. Old habits, you know."

"Yes, of course," I said. "Well, give your family my best."

"And you tell your friend Daisy that the two of you are welcome to come up for dinner any time you like. We'd love to see you both."

I half wondered how much of the invitation was Richard's doing, and how much of it was Donna and the kids who wanted us to come over, but I put a smile into my voice and said, "Oh, we'd love that too, but Daisy's schedule is so irregular right now since she's working on a big picture. We'll let you know when things settle down a bit." It was our usual excuse for social engagements that wound up being more awkward than pleasant—people were happy to have those two nice girls who shared a house as their friends, but things often were more strained if they had a real sense of us being a couple. Even in Las Capas, where relationships took all sorts of unusual forms, not everyone was on board with changes in the acceptance of what some considered immoral.

After I hung up, I thought about my other options. I'd need to make the drive over to the studio soon, so my investigations for the day were drawing to a close. Tomorrow, I could go down to check out the bay, but at this point, if they were dredging for a body, there wouldn't be much for me to investigate. I might have to wait until that process reached its conclusion before I could learn much more. But I could talk to Daisy about Archie and Clarisse visiting the set, and maybe she'd have some thoughts about Seacrest Studios and the Martinellis, too.

~

I whipped up a quick dinner when we got back from the studio while Daisy took a catnap, and after I woke her, she sat down to the meal with vigor. "I think someone gave half of craft services the week off!"

"Things are moving forward, then?" I asked.

"Sort of. They've rearranged the shooting schedule to put all of Warren's scenes on hold." She shrugged. "I guess they're trying to figure out how much we're going to have to reshoot if they find a new leading man. Or they might just adjust the script. No one's made any definitive decisions, that's for sure."

"Well, they haven't found any bodies yet, either," I said.

Daisy gasped. "Really? That could explain why there hasn't been anything about a funeral yet."

"What have folks been saying?"

"It's mostly just been gossip. If Warren was on the boat, who was he with, who would have wanted to see him dead, so on and so forth?"

"Any names popping up as major suspects?"

"Oh, am I an informant now?" Daisy asked, grinning and wiggling her eyebrows.

"Well, you're in a place where I haven't been yet."

"We can fix that," Daisy suggested. "Tomorrow's Friday, and I've only got a background shot. You could tag along with me."

I nodded. "That might be a good plan. Speaking of, Clarisse Glenn mentioned she and her brother were on set on Friday. Did you happen to run into them?"

"I heard Warren had guests on set, but no, I didn't get to meet them."

"That's a shame. I'd be interested to see what you thought of them."

"I could have gotten the clue to break this case wide open, right at the start!" she said with a delighted laugh.

"You may still, darling. So what would I be walking into if I come with you tomorrow. What's the word at the studio?"

"Well, Warren's the only person that's turned up dead, or at least missing—none of the other principal cast was on the boat with him for certain, and it seems like none of the supporting cast was either. So that was a relief to hear."

I nodded. "The police had divers in the bay today." I couldn't see out the kitchen windows to the bay from the table, but I had been keeping an eye on things while I cooked, and it seemed the divers had already finished up for the day. "I probably won't hear anything about the results until tomorrow, though."

Daisy shrugged. "Maybe no news is good news?"

"Maybe. So, people wanted him out of the picture?"

"Literally, in some cases. There are a couple of big-wigs at the studio who aren't fans. There's a Brit who wanted the leading role, too—Percy Clement."

"Never heard of him."

"No, he's more of an art house film actor. He's trying to break out of being typecast and into the American film scene. But he doesn't seem like the murdering kind."

I chuckled. "Most people who are murderers don't seem like they are. That's how they keep from getting caught."

"There are also all kinds of horrible rumors about Warren. Drugs, gambling, maybe even prostitutes or something."

I frowned, connecting these possibilities to what Miss Lewis had mentioned about the Martinellis and Seacrest Studios. "Mob ties, you think?"

Daisy shook her head. "I honestly don't believe any of the rumors about him, Sarah. I know he's an actor, and he's meant to make people believe his roles, but I've known plenty of actors who have wandered down the paths of darker vices." She shook her head a second time. "He's not one of them."

"I believe you on that count. But that doesn't mean he can't still be tied up with the mob somehow."

"Debt, maybe," Daisy said. "He's big on having the latest fashions—trend-setting, even. I imagine a lot of designers just hand him their pieces to wear, on account of his celebrity. But his lifestyle is lavish outside of that. Lots of cars. Nice cars."

"Hmm, nice cars could mean a mechanic, who might have worked on his boat, too." Instinctively, I pawed at the table looking for my pen and notebook, then realized they were in the other room.

"Go on," Daisy said. "Just means I'm getting myself a second helping of this meatloaf, and there's nothing you can do to stop me."

"I'm glad you tolerate my lousy cooking," I said as I gave her a quick peck on the cheek on my way to the living room. I brought my notepad and pen back to the table, having written myself a note to look into Warren Glenn's mechanic. "Anything else you can think of, gossip-wise?"

"Well, Percy isn't his only rival. He's just the first one I thought of, since they've been doing this whole macho posturing thing on set. And let me tell you, if you've never seen an upper-class Brit and a suave American sniping at one another, you've missed out."

That made me chuckle. "Have you forgotten how much time I spent in Europe after the War? I've seen plenty of posturing Brits, Americans, and every other nationality you can think of."

"I like to think Percy and Warren were taking it to the next level."

"Then I'll be sure to want to talk to Percy tomorrow," I replied. "You sure it won't be odd to have me on set?"

"Nah, it'll be fine. Everyone always wants me to bring you around to parties and things." She paused, sighing. "They're a little less fussy than some of your friends, Sarah."

"I don't doubt that in the slightest." I paused. "Say, you don't know if Warren had anyone in his life, do you?"

Daisy shook her head. "If he does, he keeps it well under wraps. He's taken some of the girls out, like I said, on his boat, or to dinner, or whatever. But it never seems to be more than once or twice. And everyone says he's always the most perfect gentleman."

I chewed at my lip, considering all the information I'd accumulated today. I needed to talk to Clarisse Glenn about some of the new facts, but I thought I might have to try her again in the morning, since I hadn't heard that she'd called me back at the office. I'd need to talk to Jimmy, too, to find out what the divers might have found. But I doubted Daisy would keep me at the studio all day tomorrow, so I'd squeeze those calls in when I had a chance.

Daisy waved her hand in front of my face. "You still with me, Sarah?"

I started, but then smiled at her. "Yes, sorry, just thinking things through."

"Then I suppose you don't want a second slice of meatloaf?" She gestured at my plate, still laden with my first helpings of everything.

"No, thank you. I'll scarf this down so you can get to the dishes."

"Take your time, dearest." She smiled at me, her expression kind and patient. "Dishes can wait."

CHAPTER FOUR

———

Even with Daisy at my side, I felt a little out of place at Seacrest Studios. I was tangentially connected to the film industry, and this was the first case that had brought me onto a film set. It was a bustling mass of people, similar to the way D.C. had always been busy, but the people here had a visible direction to their hurry, as they carried boxes and cables and any manner of other things to and fro.

Daisy linked her arm through mine and led me away from the primary center of activity, decorated to look like a sidewalk café similar to the patio seating at Reginald's. Off to the side, a few people congregated near tables laid out with a variety of fruit and pastries, with large carafes for beverages.

"You want anything?" Daisy asked, inclining her head toward the table.

"They just feed you all day? How on earth do you ever have an appetite when you get home?"

Daisy shrugged. "Acting's hard work. Isn't that right, Percy?"

A man in his late 40s, slender, with angular features and the beginnings of a widow's peak, turned to regard the two of us. He wore a white linen suit with a contrasting sky-blue vest, and a wildly patterned ascot that seemed to contain every color of the rainbow, and perhaps some not found in nature. "Hardly, my dear Miss Dean." His gaze flickered toward me, and he smiled. "You must be her darling friend, Sarah."

I extended my hand to him. "I am indeed. Sarah Castile. Pleasure to make your acquaintance."

"Percy Clement." He took my hand but brushed his dry lips across my knuckles rather than shaking it. "And may I say the pleasure is entirely mine."

I listened to the accent that peeked out of a few of his vowels. "Is that a Yorkshire accent I hear?"

"Well spotted! That's not one most Americans pick up in a jiff."

I smiled broadly. "I spent some years in Europe, during and after the War. Not as much time in the north of England as I might have liked, but the accent brings back memories."

Daisy released my arm. "I'll leave the two of you to chat. I've got to get into wardrobe."

"First time on set, Miss Castile?" Percy asked.

"How did you guess?"

"You look like you're afraid the whole place will burn down if you touch the wrong thing." He extended an arm to me. "Since your darling has a far more tedious wardrobe to deal with than I will, might I offer you a little tour?"

"Thank you, yes, so long as you don't mind ignorant questions about what all this hubbub is about."

Percy shrugged. "Not much hubbub today, to be honest. I'm sure you heard our leading man is ... well, out of the picture, I'd daresay."

"Yes, I had heard that."

"Well, the studio is still sorting out what's to be done about that mess, which means I'm not even certain why I'm here today. Oh, a few sips of coffee and some meaningful glances, I suppose, but the principal action has been delayed until they make a decision."

I tilted my head to the side. "You know, Daisy's been working on this film, but I'm not sure I know what it's about. I've helped her practice her lines, but they haven't given me much of the story."

"Well, that's because the story is a bit convoluted, to be honest. I'm still not sure whether my character and Mr. Glenn's are actual school chums or if that's just a convenient excuse for my accent."

"Oh!" I furrowed my brow. "And where does Daisy's role fit in to this?"

"She's the confidant of the female lead. One might say she's my counterpart. Only in the case of Mr. Glenn and myself, the script has us arguing more than agreeing, fighting over the affection of said female lead." He shrugged vaguely. "Typical male rivalry."

"And were you and Mr. Glenn rivals off-screen, Mr. Clement?"

He chuckled. "Hardly. We were colleagues, and it is a shame he's gone so soon."

"Oh," I said, tilting my head. "I'd heard gossip that suggested otherwise."

"There's always gossip, my dear Miss Castile. I suppose there was some talk when Seacrest brought me in that perhaps I'd be given the leading role. But we Brits aren't quite the right sort of palatable to American audiences—" He trailed off, and when he spoke again, had affected the more posh accent spoken by upper-class Brits. "—unless we sound like the Queen herself." He chuckled and reverted to his more natural way of speaking. "Frankly, if I were to star in an American film, it wouldn't be this one."

I laughed softly. "Well, I do hope you find some parts of being here to your liking."

"Well enough, I suppose. But I'll tell you, if I'm going to stay in this city much longer, I'm going to have to hire a driver of my own. Do you drive, Miss Castile?"

"I do, but I learned in the big cities on the East Coast. A bit different than driving here."

"It's ghastly compared to the driving in London," Percy said. "I'll tell you this much, that's the one thing I envied Mr. Glenn for. He has ... err, had, I suppose, one of the best drivers from England that money could buy."

"Did he now?"

"Oh, yes. A younger man who got his start driving for Vera Lancaster—do you know her? You might have seen something of hers after the War?"

"I'm afraid I didn't have much time for films when I was in Europe." I cast a glance in the direction Daisy had gone. "To be honest, I hadn't much interest in films until I came to Las Capas and met Daisy. She's opened my eyes to their merits."

Percy chuckled, understanding my subtlety. "Well, Miss Castile, if you and Miss Dean are ever in need of some quality entertainment, you should see if any of the theatres are showing some of the old silent films from between the Wars. That's where you're certain to find Miss Lancaster in her prime."

"Thank you for the tip, Mr. Clement." I paused. "This may seem like an odd question, but Mr. Glenn's chauffeur, do you happen to know his name?"

"Basil," he answered. "Though I couldn't tell you if the man has a last name. He's always just been Basil. 'Come along, Basil.' 'Let's go home, Basil.'" He chuckled. "Almost like calling a dog along. Not to say that Mr. Glenn didn't treat his chauffeur well. In fact, he may have set the standards too high for a lonely Brit like myself to find an adequate driver to navigate this city for me."

I patted Percy's arm. "Oh, I'm certain you can find a driver who would be willing to be lavished with attention and good will, and who could get you anywhere you needed to be in Las Capas." I paused. "Daisy sometimes has the studio send a car around for her. Do they do the same for the other actors, or only the ladies?"

Percy nodded, though his lips were a tight line. "They can and do." His gaze left my face and fixed on a point somewhere behind me. "Whether they *will* is another matter entirely."

Before I could ask him any further questions, he released my arm and stepped past me, as though he was shielding me from whatever might be happening behind my back.

"They need you in the office," a gruff voice shouted.

"Whatever for?" Percy asked. "My scene isn't for another hour."

I peeked around Percy's shoulder to spot whoever was yelling at him. The man was roughly the size and shape of a refrigerator, stuffed into a suit that might have looked reasonable on another man. In his case, it looked as though his tailor had given up at "good enough." His face was beet red, shining through the sparse stubble of his buzz cut.

"Who's this?" I murmured to Percy.

"Chet Thomas, consultant to the studio," Percy whispered. "And a pretentious pain in my backside, pardon the expression, Miss Castile."

"I'm just passing on a message, Clement," Chet barked. "Don't shoot the damn messenger." His gaze flickered in my direction, and he seemed to realize there was a woman present. "Oh, pardon me, ma'am."

I chuckled softly. "I spent more than a decade around the military, but people still think I've never heard foul language." I murmured to Percy as I stepped into view.

"My dear, you don't need to get involved with this detestable man," Percy said. "I do hope I'll get a chance to speak with you further. But duty calls." He strode away toward Chet.

I wanted to follow, but doing so would obliterate whatever cover I might have. Thus far, it looked like I'd tagged along with

Daisy. I needed to keep my investigation quiet if I was going to maintain that ruse.

Percy passed by Chet, though I could tell the two men exchanged some quiet words as they passed.

As Percy continued toward the direction Chet had indicated, Chet's voice thundered after him. "If the film flops, it's not going to look good for me, either!"

"And whose fault is that?" Percy asked, his words dripping with venom. "How am I supposed to be a foil to someone *who's not even here*?"

Chet laughed. "Yeah, you're right—his acting was what carried the scenes. You're nothing on your own." Smirking, he turned his gaze back toward me. "Remind me who you are again, sweetheart?"

I arched an eyebrow at him. "I'm sorry, what?"

"Look, just trying to keep track of what's going on here, and I don't remember you."

"That's because I'm just visiting. I'm Sarah Castile, Daisy Dean's roommate."

"Huh," he said, striding toward me and giving me a once over that felt far more invasive than it needed to, like he was eyeballing a well-marbled steak.

I did not like this man.

He extended his hand to me. "Charles Thomas. My friends call me Chet."

"And what is it you do here, Mr. Thomas?" I asked, coolly ignoring his offered hand.

He stuffed his hands into his pockets. "I'm a consultant the studio brought in for this project. Helping to make sure the film fits the writer's vision."

"Does it, then?"

He shrugged. "Not entirely, I'm afraid. And Mr. Clement and I have different visions, too. He sees himself as a leading man. I don't."

"Daisy mentioned something about needing to replace the leading man, though, on account of Mr. Glenn's accident?"

"No loss, there," Chet said, chuckling. "That is, I'm not one to say he had it coming, but he didn't fit with the writer's vision either. At least not from where I'm standing."

"Oh? Why's that?"

"For this film, the leading man has to be someone of more ambiguous morals. Warren doesn't fit the part."

"I didn't realize his morals were so vile."

"Not that, the opposite, really. He's far too much of a knight in shining armor. Too much of a do-gooder."

I knew enough about Warren Glenn's reputation to have a silent laugh at that description. No one would characterize the man about town as a do-gooder. Invincible Man, on the other hand, was a knight in shining armor to many inhabitants of Las Capas and Cerulean City as a whole. It seemed as though perhaps Chet Thomas knew Warren Glenn's secret.

I wasn't sure how much I should press that bit of information, and I didn't want to let on that I knew, so I shifted the subject a few degrees. "Well, then that boat accident is true tragedy, if we've lost a white knight."

"Eh, that damned boat was half of Warren's problem. He spends more time working on that thing than anything else. If he'd focus more on his career instead, he'd see where he's lacking. But no, he's always worrying about getting it 'ship shape' for his important guests."

"Oh, was he entertaining someone in particular?"

"He'd talked about it in the vaguest of terms. Something about a wealthy older woman who was going to join him on his boat this weekend." Chet shook his head. "Probably looking to get her to leave her money to whatever his latest charity venture is."

I wasn't aware of any of Warren Glenn's charitable leanings, but perhaps that was something to look into, as well as whoever this guest might have been. I suspected that if a wealthy society matron of Las Capas had been on the boat when it exploded, we would have heard about it already. If he was instead preparing for her visit, then whoever had set up the explosion might not have wanted Warren Glenn speaking to whoever this mystery woman was. This added yet another layer to the case.

Chet looked at me, brow creased. "What was it you said you do, Miss Castile?"

"I didn't." I smiled. "But my family is in the newspaper business."

Chet's composure slipped, his face turning bright red as he realized what he'd said, and what I'd just implied. "Uh, we don't allow the press on an active film set, Miss Castile."

"Oh, don't worry. I'm not press. I just like to keep people on their toes." I winked at him and strode away, leaving him to steam like an overboiled kettle.

CHAPTER FIVE

By Saturday morning, I was no closer to figuring out who might have murdered Warren Glenn nor where Archie Glenn had gone. And while I'd gotten some interesting information at the studio, it didn't put together any more of the puzzle.

I still hadn't been able to reach Clarisse Glenn, either, despite calling her twice on Friday, and once already after waking up. Every time I called, she was either out or not picking up the phone. So I hadn't had a chance to ask her any more questions, nor share my progress, scant though it was, with her.

"Any plans for the day?" Daisy asked while we ate breakfast.

"Perhaps. You?"

"We're shooting this afternoon. Re-shooting, maybe." She shook her head. "It's more up in the air after yesterday than it was when we got to the studio. Chet was in meetings with the director and the studio execs for half the day, and they still haven't sorted anything out."

"Out of curiosity, Does Chet treat everyone like they're a piece of meat?"

Daisy chuckled. "Everyone female."

"He wasn't fond of Warren. Or Percy. Probably not too fond of me now either."

"What did you do?" Daisy asked, her eyes widening.

"I asked him a lot of questions, and then mentioned my family's business when he asked what I did. Just to toy with him, of course. I get the impression he's used to getting his way, and I wasn't about to give it to him."

"You're wicked, Sarah," she replied, but her smirk told me she meant it in the best possible way.

"If you're working today, then, I suppose I will too."

"Which way are you headed?"

"First Precinct, for starters."

"I'll drop you off there," she said. "Maybe I'll do a little legwork myself."

"Oh?" I arched an eyebrow.

"I've got some ideas. Don't worry, nothing dangerous. But my makeup call isn't until noon, so there's no sense wasting the whole day."

"Then I'll look forward to hearing what you find out later tonight."

~

Daisy dropped me off at the First Precinct, and I smiled and waved my way past the weekend crew to Jimmy Cooper's office.

He looked up from his newspaper. "Back so soon, Miss Castile?"

"Any word on the body?"

"The divers are still in the bay. Chief says we can give it through the weekend, and then we have to go with missing, presumed dead."

"And then we'd have two missing Glenn brothers."

Jimmy nodded. "We contacted the Denver PD, and they've stopped by Archie Glenn's apartment. It appears he didn't head back home."

"So Clarisse was right. Has she been in contact with the precinct?"

"No, but that doesn't surprise me. We weren't hospitable to her."

"I can't get ahold of her either."

That made Jimmy sit up a little straighter. "You think she's missing too, now?"

I pursed my lips and shook my head. "I'm not quite ready to say so. I may just have lousy timing. But when I talked to her initially, she said something about the mob. I'm guessing no one here's done much digging into that possibility?"

"Not yet, no," he said. "What did she have to say on that front?"

"Photos, money, and blackmail. Or so she overheard."

Jimmy's jaw clenched. "You're thinking Razzi?"

Anthony Razzi, better known as Papa Razzi, was, as his nickname suggested, a photographer with ties to the mob. I knew his involvement went deeper than just "ties"—he was a Don for the Fontanellis, not the Martinellis Miss Lewis had mentioned. But the mix-up was an easy one, especially for someone who didn't have their finger on the pulse of the Las Capas underworld. And while my own fingers had strayed from that pulse in recent months, I still knew that when the words "photos" and "blackmail" popped up, it was a rare day that "Papa Razzi" didn't follow soon after.

"If the shoe fits," I said.

"I can get a warrant and talk to him this afternoon."

"I'd like to come along."

Jimmy shook his head. "No way, Sarah. I'm not letting you get involved if Razzi's involved."

"This isn't your case, it's mine. LCPD isn't even working this as a case. How are you going to get a warrant?"

"There's plenty of other reasons to get a warrant on any Fontanelli," he said, scoffing.

"And you're going to get information on the Glenn case with a warrant for a different case?"

"What's your suggestion, then?"

"No warrant. Just a friendly visit."

Arching his eyebrow, Jimmy asked, "You think that'll make him talk?"

I had to figure out how to phrase what I knew so as to not give away Warren's secrets. "Warren had a restraining order against Razzi. They've had some bad blood between them over the years. If you go in making it look like there's an LCPD case, and he's a person of interest, he'll talk. He'll disclaim all responsibility. And maybe, if we're lucky, he'll talk so much he lets something slip." I shrugged. "I've seen him do it before. Surprised he gets to keep his position with the Fontanellis with the number of times he's let things slip."

"And how are we going to explain your presence?"

"Wig and a pair of glasses, and I'm the weekend secretarial pool," I said, smiling coyly. "I do know shorthand, after all."

~

I looked odd with blonde hair, but between that and the glasses, I'm not sure my own mother would have recognized me. Of course, she didn't have the best eyesight, nor had she seen me in half a dozen years. Papa Razzi didn't blink when Jimmy and I sauntered into his office.

"Detective Cooper, how can I help you?" he asked, spreading his arms in a welcoming gesture.

Jimmy glanced at me. "My secretary, Dolores."

"Pleased to meet ya, doll."

I smiled politely, even though I wanted to scream every time someone called me doll, sweetheart, or any other terms of affection that were widespread in Las Capas. Funny how those terms were only ever applied to women, wasn't it? I took a seat near Papa Razzi's desk, notebook and pencil in hand, and looked up at Jimmy with a quick nod.

He probably saw the seething rage in my gaze, but he didn't say anything about it, just turned to Papa Razzi and began talking. "You might have heard about Warren Glenn's boating accident?"

"If by 'accident,' you mean it went boom out in the bay?" Papa Razzi chuckled. "Yeah, I heard."

"Heard anything else?"

"Afraid not. Me and Warren, we didn't get along so good, but I steered clear of him, on account of that restraining order he filed. You should have records of that, right, Detective Cooper?"

"Of course. Can you tell me your whereabouts on the evening of the twentieth?"

Papa Razzi cocked his head to the side. "Are you questioning me?"

"This is strictly a social call," Jimmy said. "We're just chatting with a few of Mr. Glenn's known associates."

"I'd hardly call myself that," Papa Razzi said, chuckling. "Man wouldn't give me the time of day."

"Nonetheless, we're just doing our due diligence. So, whereabouts?"

"Not in town, I'm afraid. You were lucky to catch me in today, to be honest. I've been working out of town all week. Just popped back in to catch up on a few things before I take my nephew fishing this afternoon."

Jimmy nodded. "I assume, then, you've got people who will vouch for your presence out of town?"

"Of course, Detective Cooper. I got a whole list of people who were out to dinner with me on the twentieth. That should be enough?"

"Sure, that should do. Can I ask what your work out of town was?"

Papa Razzi smiled like a cat that had swallowed a canary. "Fashion shoot. For an up and coming design company."

"Does that company have a name?"

"Not at liberty to disclose. It's on the up and up, but it's also hush hush, if you get my drift."

I refrained from rolling my eyes, but I dug the tip of my pencil into my notebook hard enough that it snapped. "Pencil sharpener?" I asked, my voice pitched higher and quieter than normal.

Papa Razzi plucked a pencil from his desk and held it out toward me. I had to rise to get it, and I felt his gaze on me the whole time, even though I focused on the pencil.

"You're a real looker, Dolores," he murmured as I took the pencil from his grip.

I tried to force a blush, and apparently my face flushing with anger sufficed, as he chuckled.

"Real looker," he said to Jimmy.

"Right. If you could make that list of folks you were at dinner with, we can be on our way."

Before Papa Razzi said anything more, the door to his office flew open. "Tony, they recovered the boat!"

Papa Razzi bristled, and I twisted in my chair to see who had brought us this delightful piece of news.

The man in the doorway was slack-jawed and coated in a fine sheen of sweat, his gaze darting between Jimmy, Papa Razzi, and me. He was tall and lanky, dark haired and well-tanned, wearing his shirt sleeves rolled up and his tie loose, with no jacket in evidence. I recognized him as Angelo Fontanelli, one of the family's enforcers.

And based on the way his gaze stuck to me, he saw through my disguise.

"Ah, shit. She ain't no secretary, she's a PI," Angelo said before bolting from the room.

"After you?" Jimmy asked as we both rose from our chairs.

"We'll be back with more questions," I said as I ran out of the room.

"Bring a warrant!" Papa Razzi shouted in our wake.

The door at the end of the hallway, in the direction Angelo had run, was swinging shut, a faint glimpse of daylight beyond it. I ran toward the door, wishing I had my bow and arrows with me. But while it was viable for the Huntsman to galivant around Europe with a guitar case concealing her weaponry, modern-day Las Capas allowed me to carry a pistol or nothing. So I reached into my bag and unholstered my M1917.

"Sarah, what have I told you about carrying a gun?" Jimmy grumbled behind me.

"Detective Cooper, I know my rights as a citizen of the United States and the State of California. And I do know how to use my weapon."

"I thought you were a nurse in the War? And the Huntsman is an archer."

"I was a nurse, and an archer, for that matter, but that doesn't mean I didn't learn how to handle a gun," I replied. "Also, I'm not the Huntsman anymore. But don't worry, I don't intend to shoot him, no matter how much I'd like to, unless he opens fire first."

I burst through the door and scanned the area for Angelo Fontanelli, who was nowhere in sight. In the distance, I heard tires squealing. I headed toward the street, fumbling through the elaborate garden on this side of Papa Razzi's house, startling several gardeners as I went. Jimmy followed me.

Pushing through the hedgerow, my wig snagged in the branches, and I let it fall from my head. A dark sedan took a wide right-hand turn at the end of the road, far enough away that I could see neither the plates nor the driver. For all I knew, it could have been any other reckless driver, not Angelo Fontanelli.

Jimmy joined me on the sidewalk, my bedraggled wig in hand. "Lost him?"

"Lost him." I tucked the wig into my handbag, not bothering to try to maintain the ruse of my cheap disguise.

"Alright, I need to head back to the station for a warrant. Seems like the Fontanellis might know a little bit more about this boat accident than Razzi was letting on."

I nodded. "I'll catch up with you later. I'm going to see if I can find anyone who might have seen where Angelo went."

"Be careful, Sarah." Jimmy glanced at my service revolver. "And keep that in your bag, please."

I slipped the gun back into the holster I'd attached near the top of my bag for easy access in a hurry. "Yes, Detective. Good luck."

"Yeah, you too."

CHAPTER SIX

Strolling down the sidewalk in Papa Razzi's neighborhood, I heard snippets of conversation from the neighbors' porches. My memories drifted back to the days I'd spent in small Italian villages, learning more of the language there than I'd ever learned in my book studies. And The Venetian—one of the most unusual heroes I'd met in my time in Europe—teaching me some of the more colorful Italian swear words he'd learned over his long centuries.

Some of those words were even the same words I heard ahead of me now.

An older man was hunched over the edge of his yard, where wide tire tracks marred the once perfect grass of his lawn. He poked at the damaged terrain with a cane, grumbling and cursing under his breath.

"Good morning, sir," I said in Italian. "I'm looking for information about the man who drove across your lawn?"

"Ruined my lawn, you mean. That was Angelo Fontanelli. He's nothing but trouble for this street." He jerked his chin toward the Fontanelli house. "All of them. Trouble."

"I don't suppose you saw where Mr. Fontanelli went?"

He gestured toward the stop sign where I'd seen the sedan take the wide right. "Toward Main Street. Probably going to go drink all day, like he does every day."

"Is there anything else he tends to do with his days? Is he a braggart around this street?"

The old man chuckled. "Oh, yes, he is. Always talking about his fancy car and fancy threads and fancy guns. And the fancy women he says he's going to go on dates with."

I inclined my head slightly to the side, hoping to tease out a bit more of Angelo's bragging. "Does he ever talk about any of the film actors? Like Warren Glenn?"

"Warren Glenn?" The old man crossed himself. "God rest his soul. My wife loves all his films. He seemed like a nice enough boy, even when he was coming around here. Always respectful to all of us on the street, even if he was here to visit them." He jerked his chin toward the Fontanelli house again.

"What was he doing at their house, I wonder?" I asked, trying to sound dumbfounded.

The old man looked around to make sure no one was listening to us, and he whispered, "He made some bad horse bets. Had to come here to pay his debts."

Horse bets didn't sound like the Warren Glenn I knew, but I wondered if maybe the Fontanellis had been extorting him for something else, and he let the neighbors think it was horse racing. Either way, I wasn't sure it made a lot of sense for the Fontanellis to be involved in the explosion. A dead man couldn't repay debts, horse racing ones or otherwise.

"Anyway, that Angelo didn't like Mr. Glenn," the old man continued. "Said he couldn't ... ah, what's the English expression?" He cleared his throat and spoke in heavily accented English. "Act his way out from paper bag?"

I chuckled and returned to Italian. "Yes, but 'of' a paper bag. I've heard a few people say that, but I must admit, I'm a fan, like your wife. I thought he was a fine actor."

"Eh. He was alright. He always had the pretty girls flocking to him, so I like to watch his films with my wife." He looked down at his yard again and sighed. "Nice to talk to you, miss. I need to fix my lawn now. Damn Angelo."

"Good luck," I said. With the man's mention of Main Street in mind, I headed in that direction, ready to check out whatever bar Angelo might have ducked into to evade Jimmy and me.

~

By the time I reached the third bar on Main Street, my feet were beginning to ache. I stopped at a pay phone to call Daisy, since she had the car at the studio lot. If she wouldn't be there much longer,

I could take a cab to the lot. If she anticipated being most of the day, I might take a cab home instead.

"Suncrest Studios, this is Margery speaking, how may I direct your call?"

"Hi, Margery, this is Sarah Castile. I was hoping to speak with Daisy Dean." Margery had been at Suncrest for long enough to recognize my name and know I wasn't just a fan calling to talk to Daisy.

"Oh, sure! Give me just a couple of minutes to track her down."

I watched the sidewalks and street while I waited, looking to see if I spotted Angelo or any other Fontanellis. But the midday crowd seemed to be primarily families out for a stroll or shopping, not mob enforcers getting drunk. Maybe the old man had been wrong about where Angelo did his drinking, or maybe Angelo had decided he needed to flee farther than his usual watering holes.

The line crackled, followed by Daisy's voice. "Sarah, are you alright?"

"I'm fine, Daisy, but thank you for the concern. Just wondering if I should get a cab to the studio or home."

"Neither, actually." After a brief pause, she asked, "Have you got something to write on?"

"Always. What's going on?"

"The tires on the car looked a little low this morning, so I went down to the marina mechanic to have them checked out."

"Marina mechanic? Why not just go to the service station?"

"Because the marina mechanic had Warren's boat in his shop for about a week before the explosion, and it's back there now," Daisy said softly. Louder, she continued, "You'll want to go see Clyde Brown on Seaside Boulevard to pick up the car, alright? And then you can swing by the studio. I should be done by then."

I caught on to what Daisy was doing. Someone was listening to her on the phone, but she'd left the car at a place where I could get some more clues on the case. "Wonderful, darling, I'll see you soon."

"You flatterer," she giggled, always amused when I called her pet names on the phone, out of earshot of her co-workers. "I'll see you when you get here."

~

45

It was easy enough to find the marina mechanic on Seaside, with a large sign outside reading "Brown's Marina Repairs." And our car was parked out front, too. I paid the cabbie and hopped out.

A black man in his fifties, wearing grease stained coveralls and a cap over his graying hair, met me outside the front door. "You Miss Castile?"

"Yes, Mr. Brown, I suppose?"

"You can call me Clyde, ma'am."

"Then call me Sarah." I glanced at the car. "Thanks for indulging Miss Dean with a tire top-off."

"Oh, there wasn't anything wrong with your tires, Sarah. That Miss Dean's a fine actress, isn't she?"

"Yes, she is. Did she tell you what's going on, then?"

Clyde nodded. "C'mon inside, and I'll show you the paperwork."

I couldn't be certain if he meant actual paperwork or if this was his way of removing us from the prying eyes of passersby, but I followed him all the same.

The inside of the garage reeked of smoke, and as my eyes adjusted to the dim interior, I saw the reason for that. The remnants of Warren Glenn's boat lay on one side of the garage space. The craft was smaller than I expected, and also in many more pieces than I'd realized it would be in. Still visible under a layer of soot was the name of the boat. *Invincible*. I refrained from laughing aloud at both the audacity and the potential irony of the name.

"Mr. Glenn brought his boat in about a week before the accident. He picked her up bright and early on Wednesday morning. I can show you the records of my repairs. There shouldn't have been anything wrong with her."

"Did he pick it up himself?"

Clyde nodded. "He was here, yes. Him and his driver, Basil. But they brought a truck and its driver too, because Mr. Glenn's car isn't equipped to tow a boat like his."

"Did you know the driver, or the company he worked for?"

"Not personally, no. I've seen him around, though. He drives for the marina itself, and the people who have berths there can use his truck to take their boats where they need to be."

"When Mr. Warren dropped off his boat, did he give you specific things he needed worked on?"

"Normally, yes, but not this time. This time he just said he needed her to be all shipshape before Friday—yesterday, that is. There wasn't much of anything for me to fix, but I did as he asked."

"Did he say why he needed her shipshape?"

"No, he didn't. If I had to guess, I'd say he and Basil might have had some plans to take her out over the weekend." Clyde paused and shook his head. "Poor Basil. He was devoted to Mr. Glenn. I can only imagine how distraught he must be."

I nodded, the wheels in my mind turning. Where was Basil? Had he been on the boat with Warren? The divers still hadn't retrieved any bodies from the bay. Would they find one or two?

"So Mr. Glenn picked up the boat early Wednesday, had her driven to the marina, and then within what, say a dozen hours, she had exploded?"

"That sounds about right, yes."

"Which means someone with access to the marina had about twelve hours in which to tamper with the boat. Thank you, Clyde, you've been most helpful. Ah, may I pay you for your time working with Miss Dean and our car?"

He shook his head. "Miss Dean already took care of it. Let me know if I can be any more help to either of you ladies."

"Thank you, Clyde. Have a good afternoon."

~

Daisy met me at the edge of the parking lot when I reached the studio, her face pale and drawn.

"Are you alright?" I asked.

"The picture might be shutting down entirely," she said, her voice quiet and strained.

"Oh, no." I embraced her, and she leaned into the hug. "They haven't found a new star?"

She shook her head against my shoulder. "They're saying there isn't enough footage to piece in Warren for the other parts, but there's too much footage to reshoot the whole thing with a different actor. There's a lot of grumbling all over the place, and I guess the writer has even deigned to set foot on set. Chet's being an absolute nightmare, goading me about my press connections."

"I'm sorry I poked at him with that, Daisy."

"Oh, I don't blame you one bit," she said, pulling away from me. She wiped her eyes and smiled. "He deserves it. My only consolation is that if I wind up out of a job, so will he. But it's much easier for me to find a new project than it will be for a consultant."

I gestured behind Daisy with my chin. "It looks like a bunch of people are gathering over there. Should you join them?"

"Yeah, this may be the word we're all waiting for." Daisy squeezed my hand and then walked back toward the set, joining her co-workers.

Chet glanced in Daisy's direction when she rejoined the group, and then looked toward me, his nostrils flaring. Even as someone stepped onto a raised surface, Chet stormed away from the group, heading directly toward me.

"Miss Castile," he said, a sneer marring his face. "Of Castile Investigations, I presume."

"Oh, yes, that's me alright."

"What in the hell do you think you're doing here?"

"Picking up my roommate, once she knows what's happening with the film." I glanced over his shoulder. "Shouldn't you be over there doing the same?"

"I already know. They're taking a different direction, rewriting the script. My client and I won't be here much longer. So there's nothing more for you to pry into where I'm concerned."

"Who said I was prying into you?" I asked, letting a bit of acidity color my words. "Are you a cheating husband whose wife might have hired one of the few female PIs in Las Capas to get the dirt? After all, that's the sort of cases female PIs work, isn't it?"

"You're up to something more," he spat back, showing me his bare left hand. "Not married, never have been. You're working the Glenn case. And I can assure you, I had nothing to do with that."

"Well, thank you for that assurance," I said.

"Warren Glenn was a no-talent hack who dishonored the spirit of my client's work, and the project falling apart like this is proof. He couldn't be trusted to think of anyone but himself, because he's nothing more than a money-grubbing, favor-courting fool who got what was coming to him."

"Oh, I thought before, you said he was too much of a goody-two-shoes. He seems to be a man of many facets."

"Yeah, he's like an onion. With layers. And horrible taste. Would you like me to go on?"

"Thank you, Mr. Thomas, I think that's enough." I looked past his shoulder again. "I do think the studio folks got all that, too, but you might want to go see what news they have for you."

Several of the faces I could see from my vantage point had reddened, either out of anger or embarrassment, and I wasn't sure I wanted to stick around to learn which direction Chet's face was about to go.

"Just watch whose toes you step on, Miss Castile," he snarled. "Making enemies of important people is how you wind up dead in Las Capas."

I watched him as he stomped away. His final statement hadn't been wrong. But I wasn't sure he was clear on his true level of importance. Or was he referring to someone else entirely?

CHAPTER SEVEN

———————

The good news was that the show was still on, so to speak. As Chet had said, the production would continue, just with some heavy rewriting, which would explain why Warren Glenn appeared in some scenes. "The writer was mad as hell," Daisy told me, "but at least I've still got a job. Speaking of, how's yours going?"

We'd made a quick meal of sandwiches for dinner, as neither of us was up for cooking anything more elaborate. So I told Daisy about my day around bites of my ham and Swiss on rye.

"There are a few things I keep circling back to. The first is who was Warren planning to take out on his boat?"

"Well, all the cast and crew are relieved it wasn't them, but no one seems to think it *was* going to be them, either. He'd talked about taking some of us out on his boat, but nothing solid. So it must have been someone not involved in the film."

"He had his contract at Seacrest, so it doesn't seem likely it would be one of the other studios, right?"

"Probably not," Daisy said, her mouth pursing. "I mean, unless he was trying to find someone to buy out his contract, so he could go to another studio. He wasn't a household name when he signed with Seacrest. Nowadays, he could find another studio willing to make that sort of investment in him. Some of the big names make a game of it, almost."

"Had you heard any mutterings about him jumping ship?" I chuckled softly. "Oh, that's an awful metaphor."

"No, I hadn't heard anything directly. It's just one of the things you start speculating about when someone reaches a certain level of star power."

Of course, there were half a dozen other facets of Warren Glenn's life that could have been related to his choice of person to take out on his boat. I'd barely scratched the surface of those possibilities, but some of them also weren't the sort I was going to discuss openly with Daisy. It seemed unlikely it was another of the cape and cowl set, but it could have been. But there were other options as well.

"You mentioned Anthony Razzi was doing a fashion shoot, but he wouldn't say who for?" Daisy asked, poking at a discarded crust from her sandwich.

"That's right."

"I know a few girls who might be working fashion rather than film right now. Want me to ask around?"

"If you don't mind, that would be helpful."

She nodded. "Sure, I'll see what I can dig up. So who do you have on the suspect list right now?"

"It's a little hard to say. Chet Thomas swears he wasn't involved, but I'm getting the impression he holds a pretty strong grudge against people who get in his way. I don't think he'll be inviting me to any cookouts this summer. Jimmy's working on an angle involving Angelo Fontanelli, and that's looking pretty strong. The problem is the motives don't make any sense. I can't find anyone who would have wanted Warren Glenn *dead*. Not involved in the picture, sure. But if he did owe the mob money, why would they have him killed? You can't collect from a dead man."

"If Jimmy finds Angelo, you'll at least be able to question him."

"True, but that may only eliminate him from the possible pool. I still haven't been able to get in contact with Clarisse Glenn, and no one has seen Archie Glenn either. But it doesn't make sense for Clarisse to hire me if she was involved. Archie, on the other hand? Maybe."

"Well, I suppose it's early in the case, still. I'm sure you'll sort it all out," Daisy said, rising from the table and picking up my plate.

"Oh, do you happen to know anything about Warren's driver? Name of Basil? British, I think?"

"Hmm, you know, I've seen him, picking up Warren or hanging around the set, but we've never spoken. Basil, huh? You might ask some of the other drivers, but that would have to wait until Monday."

"It's occurred to me that if he wasn't on the boat with Warren, he might have information. But all I've got is a first name, and that he used to work for an old British silent film star. What was it Mr. Clement said? Lancaster, maybe?"

"Vera Lancaster?" Daisy asked.

"That's it, yes. I take it you've heard of her?"

Daisy nodded, her eyes lighting up. "She was amazing, back in the day. Such an expressive face. She retired around the time the talkies started, though. Said that was a younger woman's game."

"So she's quite elderly, then?"

"No, I think she died a while back. Gosh, she'd be eighty or ninety by now if she's still living."

"Well, I don't know how old this Basil is now," I said, "but he apparently drove for her in England."

"Oh, that's not—" Daisy trailed off. "Well, I don't know. He's got the sort of face where he could be twenty or forty, maybe even fifty, and you wouldn't know just by seeing him."

"And how old was Warren?"

"Early thirties. A few years younger than us."

"What sort of relationship did the two of them have?" I asked.

Daisy frowned. "Now that's ... huh. When you ask the question that way, it makes me think. They're quite affectionate with one another. Strangely so, you might say, for an employer and employee." She paused, then gasped. "Do you think Warren and Basil—?"

My eyebrows shot up. I'd known Warren Glenn for two years, but in the superhero set, the question of one's sexuality only came up if someone was known to be in a relationship. And Warren never had been, to the best of my knowledge. "Well, I hadn't considered that possibility. Do you ... is Warren gay?"

Daisy nodded slowly. "He's never said as much aloud, but like I said, he only ever goes on a date or two with any of the women who manage to snare him."

"Well that adds an interesting new twist to the Archie Glenn possibility," I said glumly. "Family upset about the inclinations of their golden boy?"

"Boy, that would explain Chet, too."

"It could explain a variety of things," I murmured. Though Las Capas on the whole was more accepting of alternative sexualities, it didn't mean every resident of Las Capas felt the same way. Thinking about it always made me a little queasy, a remnant of my upbringing that would have decried a relationship between Warren and Basil just as ferociously as it would have balked at my own relationship. There were reasons I didn't speak to most of my family.

Daisy noticed my sudden shift in mood and wrapped her arms around me while planting a kiss on my cheek. "I'll see what I can find out, darling, but I hope we're wrong about his brother, or at least the reason for his involvement, if he is involved."

~

I'd planned to spend my Sunday in the garden, digging in the dirt and amongst living things, both as a way to take my mind off the case and to allow my brain to piece things together in the background. I hadn't gotten far, though, when Daisy came outside. "Sarah, there's an Ester Lopez on the phone for you."

Ester Lopez was a passing acquaintance from the superhero scene in Cerulean City, who went by the name of Pícaro. She didn't live on this side of the city, so I didn't interact with her much. She was some sort of incarnation of a Catholic saint, from my understanding, one who blessed or cursed poor Ester with visions. And it was usually those visions that led her to contact other superheroes, former or otherwise, out of the blue.

I removed my gardening gloves outside and my shoes at the door, careful to not track dirt into the freshly vacuumed living room, and picked up the waiting phone.

"Ester?"

"You're looking for Angelo Fontanelli?"

I chuckled. "That's remarkably specific for a vision."

"Not a vision this time. My cousin cleans house for an elderly Italian man who you must have talked to about Angelo. And she knows some of the people he runs with, so she wanted me to tell you where to look for him."

"This isn't anything that will get your cousin in trouble, is it?"

Ester scoffed. "No, not even a little. Angelo's a loose cannon. I don't know what you're looking for him for, but I'm sure he didn't do anything noble and upstanding. If you've got a way to get him off the streets, it's better for everyone involved."

I grabbed the pen and notepad we kept by the phone. "Alright, where did she suggest looking for him?"

~

The bars Ester's cousin had recommended were all closed on Sunday, but there was a pool hall that did slow business in the afternoon, the connected bar closed and barricaded with a stack of wooden chairs preventing any pool players from slipping over for an illicit Sunday drink. Aside from the attendant, I was the only woman in the place, so I started by approaching her.

"I'm trying to locate Angelo Fontanelli."

She gazed past me at the men playing pool, then returned her attention to me. "He's not here."

"You don't happen to know anywhere else he might frequent on a Sunday?"

"No." She shrugged. "Might be at home, sleeping off whatever mischief he got into last night."

"Does he live near here?"

"I don't know where he lives. What do you take me for, a phone book?"

I had looked Angelo Fontanelli up in the phone book before heading over here, but there wasn't anyone by that name listed, nor did I think calling the various A. Fontanellis would get me anywhere, especially as none of the addresses were on this side of the city. "I've just got a message to get to him, and I'm having the worst time finding him."

One of the pool players had made his way over to where the attendant and I were talking. "You got a message for Angelo?"

I turned and gave the young man a smile. "Yes, do you know where he lives?"

"Naw, but I can find someone to get him a message." His gaze darted to my handbag and back, implying a payment would be appreciated.

"His ears only, I'm afraid. When's the last time you saw him?"

"Thursday, maybe? Naw, Wednesday night. He came in here and shot a round with me." The man shook his head. "He smelled like he'd been working in a garage all day."

I nodded. "Yes, that's what I need to speak to him about." I reached into my handbag and rifled through a stack of business cards by touch, extracting one that identified me as a city inspector in the vaguest of ways. Handing it to the attendant, I asked, "If you see him, could you ask him to give me a call? Normal business hours are just fine. I just happened to be in the neighborhood today."

The woman looked at the card, then at the pool player, then back at me. "Yeah, sure. Will do."

I was pretty sure the card wouldn't make it to Angelo, or if it did, it would be with a strong caveat against contacting me. But I played along with the polite fiction that the attendant would help me out. "Thank you very much," I said, glancing above her at the prices for a game of pool. I extracted a quarter from my coin purse and placed it in front of her with a tilt of my head toward the man who had spoken to me. "His next game's on me."

~

A lot of businesses in Las Capas closed on Sundays, but the marina was not one of them, as popular as it was to take boats out on the bay in good weather. As I drove toward the water, hundreds of small boats dotted the shimmering surface. Some had likely launched from private docks or were small enough crafts to launch without a dock. But the majority of these boats spent their weekends on the water and their weeks docked at the marina.

A section of the bay had been demarcated with buoys and rope, with a larger boat anchored nearby. It appeared to be the base of operations for the divers, who were still working to find any remains from the explosion. I was curious to learn the results. It seemed unlikely they'd find a body for Invincible Man, though I did still wonder where he was if he hadn't been on the boat when it exploded. That none of the other superheroes in the city had heard from him seemed odd. And I knew General Justice would be quick to let me know if Invincible Man had been in contact.

I'd been to the marina once or twice, as they also rented small sailboats to those who wanted to enjoy the water without the cost of boat ownership. I'd found sailing in the bay much different than sailing in the cape near Cobalt City, but the skills I'd learned in my youth helped well enough here.

I approached the rental desk on my arrival. If Angelo had some connection to the marina, and I could prove it, I would be well on my way to making a strong case against him as the person responsible for Warren Glenn's boat explosion.

The young man at the rental counter appraised my clothing. I'd changed out of my gardening outfit and into a smart dress, but that meant I wasn't dressed for sailing, either. "Can I help you, ma'am?"

"Sorry, not here for a rental today, I'm afraid. I'm looking for Angelo Fontanelli. I think he might work here."

Shaking his head, the young man said, "No, ma'am, I don't know anyone by that name."

Somewhere nearby, someone cleared their throat, but as I glanced around, I couldn't tell where it had come from.

"Hmm, maybe he rents a slip, then?"

"I'm afraid I'm not at liberty to give out information about our customers, ma'am."

"Well, I'm just trying to track him down. He said he had a boat he was looking to sell, but the number he gave me has been disconnected, and I didn't know where else to turn. Thank you for your time."

I turned and headed back toward my car, but I walked slowly and took the longest possible route, all the while looking for whoever had cleared their throat.

My patience was rewarded when a younger man with dark hair and a matching mustache came out another door to the marina building, wearing a mechanic's coverall bearing a patch reading "Bob" and wiping his hands on a grease-stained towel.

"You need to talk to Angelo about a boat?"

I chuckled inwardly. Even though that statement was oversimplified, it was the truth. "Yes," I said. "Do you know him?"

"He's my cousin." He shook his head. "But he doesn't work here, and he doesn't have a boat to sell."

"Does he have any involvement with the marina? Might he have come to visit you at work recently?"

"No, he doesn't come down here. He sometimes has me do him some favors—drop some things off for people who keep their boats here."

I inhaled sharply, unable to avoid the tell. "What kind of things?"

"I shouldn't be talking about this."

"Listen, Bob, is it? Let me be straight with you. I'm trying to find out if there's any possibility your cousin was involved with the boat explosion the other night. If you tell me he wasn't, then there won't be any trouble."

Bob shook his head, his eyes suddenly wide with fear. "No, no way he was involved with that. It's things like money, or cigars, or fancy booze usually. Maybe some illegal things sometimes, but I try real hard not to know what I'm delivering."

I nodded. "Okay, thank you. I'm sorry I had to pry." And I was sorrier he'd punched a giant hole in my most likely theory, but I wasn't about to let that out.

"Look, don't tell anyone I told you, okay? It's hard enough when people find out my mom's maiden name was Fontanelli. I just want to do an honest job for honest pay. If it was anyone other than my cousin, I wouldn't help. But me and Angelo grew up together. He's like my brother."

"You've saved him some potential trouble, Bob. If you're sure he didn't have anything to do with the boat explosion, then I'm sure he'll be just fine." I tilted my head to the side. "If you don't mind my asking, how long have you been working at the marina?"

"Ten years or so," he said, shrugging.

"Then you must know most of the other folks who are around—other employees, the regulars, all of that?"

"Yes, ma'am."

"I don't suppose you've seen anyone around who doesn't belong here? Anyone at all?"

"Excepting yourself, ma'am?" He gave me a faint smile at that, then hesitated, his eyes narrowing. "Actually, yes. I figured he might be from one of the studios, scouting locations or something. We don't get a lot of places filming here—the old marina on the other side of the bay is better for that sort of thing. But occasionally we get newer guys, who think they've stumbled onto a gold mine with an active, working marina."

"Can you tell me what he looked like?"

Bob shrugged. "Not much of anything that could help. Tall, thin, dark haired, nicely dressed. Ah, expensive Italian leather shoes and hand rolled cigarettes?"

I nodded along with the description, realizing even with the last two specific details, Bob could have been describing a huge swath of people in Las Capas. Tall, thin, and dark haired could have been any one of my cousins back in Cobalt City, for that matter. Even the final details didn't help much—plenty of people wore Italian leather shoes and rolled their own cigarettes. I handed Bob my card anyway. "If you think of anything else, or see him around again, could you let me know?"

Bob nodded as he took my card, then glanced back toward the marina building. "I should get back inside before anyone wonders where I've gone. I hope you're right about Angelo being fine."

"I usually am," I said.

CHAPTER EIGHT

I still hadn't spoken with Clarisse Glenn since she hired me, so I started my Monday morning by taking a cab to the Grand Hotel. The sidewalk outside was crowded with people awaiting cabs, suitcases in hand as they checked out of the hotel. I made my way through the mass and into the elegant lobby, all gilt and marble.

One of the clerks at the front desk, a bright-eyed young woman, smiled at my approach. "Good morning, ma'am, how can we assist you?"

"I'm looking for Clarisse Glenn—she's a guest here."

The clerk nodded and looked at a ledger book on her side of the counter. "Ah, I'm afraid Miss Glenn *was* a guest here. She checked out this morning."

I glanced back toward the street, wondering if I'd somehow missed her in the crowd of people on the sidewalk. Turning back to the clerk, I asked, "She didn't happen to say where she was going, did she?"

"I'm afraid I wasn't working then, ma'am. She checked out quite early, 4:30 a.m."

"That's odd, isn't it?"

"It's uncommon, to be sure, but not unheard of. She had given us an indication that she was unsure how long her stay might last. It may be she was called away on whatever task led to that uncertainty."

I nodded, containing my sigh. Clarisse Glenn had been evasive since she'd hired me—at least she'd paid my entire fee upfront, for two weeks' worth of work. However, it led me to wonder what was going on. Most clients wanted regular updates on my work, or at the very least, they made sure I knew how and where to find them in case I had more questions or any breaks in the case. There was something odd going on here, just out of reach.

My expression must have been somewhere between confusion and annoyance, because the clerk continued. "Is there anything else I might assist you with today, ma'am?"

"No, thank you. Not unless she gave any sort of means of contacting her?"

"She registered an address in Denver when she checked in."

I smiled at the clerk. "Would you mind jotting that down for me? I ought to send her a note expressing my pleasure at having met her."

With a nod, the clerk pulled out a slip of paper and copied the address for me. "Have a pleasant day, ma'am."

"You as well."

~

I called the First Precinct after I got back home, asking for Detective Cooper.

"Sarah, how are you?"

"I'm well, yourself?"

"Busy."

"Any news on the search for a body?"

He let out a long sigh. "Yes, but I don't think it's what you're hoping for. The divers found a body that seems like it's at the correct level of trauma and decomposition to be our man ... or at least the victim of the boat explosion. But it's going to take the coroner at least a couple of days to confirm the identity."

"What about the chauffeur, Basil? He's someone who might be able to ID the body."

"He hasn't been seen in a few days, at least. Everyone connected to this case seems to be in the wind. I don't like it."

"Neither do I." I debated whether I should suggest that perhaps there were other people in the city who could identify Warren Glenn's body, based on his work as Invincible Man. But I wasn't certain what sort of excuse I could give as to why Richard Justice was familiar enough with an actor he'd never been seen with publicly. And I didn't think I should suggest bringing in someone like Rashimi, a local sorceress who wore the cape and cowl when needed. Magic was something I'd dealt with, but most of the police of Las Capas wouldn't be comfortable accepting. Ultimately, perhaps it was better to just let the coroner do the work in the normal fashion.

"So we've got a missing chauffeur and a missing brother," Jimmy said. I could almost hear him shaking his head over the phone.

"A missing sister, too," I added.

"Oh?"

"She checked out of her hotel at 4:30 this morning. Seems a little odd, wouldn't you say?"

"A little. I assume you questioned the staff?"

"The clerk I talked to wasn't working when Clarisse checked out. She didn't find it odd that someone would check out when most sensible people are asleep."

"Eh, it's Las Capas," Jimmy said with a chuckle. "I don't know how many sensible people live in this town. You said the sister hired you, though. Doesn't seem like she'd hire you to figure out that she arranged Warren Glenn's death."

"I agree. Honestly, I'm more worried she's gotten herself mixed up in something else."

"Archibald, though?"

"I'm less certain when it comes to him," I admitted. "Having not spoken with him complicates matters. And it seems he and Warren may have been at odds with one another. But—" I trailed off. Warren Glenn fit the description Bob had given me—tall, thin, and dark haired. If his brother looked similar to him, then Archie also fit that description. The only flaw with this theory was that Warren Glenn was well known in Las Capas and across the world. If Bob had seen a famous actor, or someone who looked a lot like him, at the marina, he would have identified him as such.

"But what, Sarah?"

I shook my head. "Never mind, it didn't pan out. Don't suppose you know anything more about the chauffeur? All I've got is a first name and that he worked in England a while ago."

"Basil Worthington, aged thirty-eight, native of England. My secretary is locating some traffic accident reports he's listed as a party to, but she said the indexes list him as the one being hit by reckless drivers, never the cause of an accident himself. Seems he's got a quite good record as a driver."

"Don't suppose those reports give an address for him?"

"They probably do. I can let you know when I get my hands on them."

"You know, this is a long shot, but could you have her see if Warren Glenn has any cases related to him on file? I know he's not in the phone book, but he's got properties in Las Capas."

"Good idea, I'll see what she can find."

"That Basil hasn't been seen for a few days is either suspicious or worrisome," I said. "I'd like to swing by some of Warren's houses and speak with whatever staff have stuck around."

"How many houses do you think this guy owns?"

"A lot, from my understanding. How recent is the most recent accident report, out of curiosity?"

"Six months ago, she said," Jimmy replied.

"Hmm. Don't suppose you know the end result of that one?"

"I can tell you the most likely outcome. It never went to court, and Warren Glenn had any charges brought against the other driver whisked away."

"Is that common?" I asked.

"When you've got that kind of money, I suppose. It's not like Warren Glenn needed to sue everyone who dinged his car. He could afford to have them fixed or replaced. So why bother taking it to court?"

"I suppose that makes sense." But the wheels in my head were always turning. Did Warren not want these cases to go to court because he was being magnanimous or because he was trying to keep these accidents out of the spotlight? Or was it Basil he wanted to keep out of the spotlight? Whichever way you sliced it, it fell into a rather interesting pattern. "Thanks for your time, Jimmy. Keep me posted on the coroner, and I'll swing by for those accident reports in a day or two."

~

Daisy was back from grocery shopping on a rare weekday off for her in time to throw together lunch, and I sat at the table while she cooked.

"So, I asked around about Papa Razzi's fashion shoot. 'Out of town' is a pretty generous depiction of the truth. It was over in Rosita Heights."

"Rosita Heights? Well, I guess that's technically not Las Capas, but it is still Cerulean City."

"Exactly."

"Did you find out whose line it was for?"

"Mm-hmm." Daisy finished dishing corned beef hash onto my plate and set the skillet back on the stove. "Gloria Graves."

"From the way you say that, I suspect you think I know who that is," I said.

Daisy's eyes widened. "How can you *not* know Gloria Graves? We've watched a couple of her movies!"

I shrugged. "Which one is she?"

Lifting a hand dramatically to her forehead, Daisy drawled, "Oh, my sweet Romeo, wherever are you?"

"That sounds like someone couldn't remember their Shakespeare."

"Well, yes, the film was a modern reinterpretation of *Romeo and Juliet*. But she was outstanding. And you've seen that one."

I nodded, having a dim recollection of watching a poorly altered version of *Romeo and Juliet* with Daisy at my side. Frankly, I recalled more about surreptitiously holding her hand than the film itself. "Well, alright, so she's in fashion now?"

"Seems that way," Daisy said around forkfuls of food. "She's been retired for a while, mostly a recluse, up in Rosita Heights. But word is she designed the line herself. Or she's got some designer willing to put her name on their work."

"Hmm," I said, sipping more of my coffee. "Well, I suppose that's Papa Razzi's alibi all sewn up. I don't think he's the sort to get his hands dirty directly anyway."

"So what's next for your case, then?"

"I'm waiting on some information from the police. Not much to do until I have that. So I suppose I'll walk down to the library later. Maybe I'll read up on this Gloria Graves, too," I said with a smile.

~

Fifteen minutes at the library was all it took for me to realize Vera Lancaster was a dead end, literally. She'd passed away eighteen years ago. Given Basil's age, he must have driven for her in her final years.

65

I didn't have the dates for the traffic accidents from Jimmy yet, but he'd mentioned the last one had been six months ago, so I flipped through the papers from last November to see if there'd been anything noted about Basil that I didn't already know.

I found an article about the accident, complete with photograph of a distraught Basil, pressed up against the shoulder of a man a few inches taller than him, the other man's arms wrapped around Basil's frame. Though the other man wasn't identified in the photograph, what little I could see of him looked like it could have been Warren Glenn. That made it all the more curious that he wasn't identified—this was the sort of thing that newspaper readers ate up, when a handsome star was seen publicly embracing his chauffeur.

I poked around at a few other papers from around the same time, and saw the same photo from a few different angles, including one credited to Anthony Razzi that showed and identified both Warren and Basil. The article in that paper was more salacious, speculating on the close relationship between the two men, though not quite reaching the point of flat out stating that their relationship was romantic or sexual. But reading between the lines, the message was clear. The paper wasn't one I cared for, but now I wondered if I ought to take a subscription of it at my office, to find the sorts of seedy reporting that might lead me to new cases.

Flipping that paper over, I noticed the back page had an article about Gloria Graves, and I picked it back up. The article talked about her forthcoming fashion line and its inspirations—the exact sort of boring drivel I didn't enjoy reading. The photograph caught my attention, though—the article said Gloria Graves was in her late 50s, but the woman in the photograph looked simultaneously older and younger than that. I examined the grainy lines of her face, certain at least some of the age shown there was achieved by the judicious application of makeup.

It was her eyes that gave it away—they were not the eyes of a woman in her fifties, but the vivacious eyes of a woman in her twenties, at best.

I tapped my chin as I considered this. Based on what little I knew of Gloria Graves, she ought to be in her late fifties, as the article suggested. The makeup giving her an older appearance may have been accidental or caused by the poor quality of the newspaper photograph. But the eyes glimmering in the midst of the face seemed out of place.

I flipped through the card catalog for more articles about Gloria Graves. As I dug through the old newsprint, I found most of them didn't include photographs at all, but they confirmed much of what I knew through Daisy—Gloria Graves had risen to prominence fifteen or twenty years ago, her main claim to fame was playing Juliet as a woman in her late thirties in the modern adaptation of *Romeo and Juliet*, and she'd retired a few years back with a quip about now only being suited to play the Nurse in any adaptation of that play.

I found a single magazine article the library had on file with glossy pages bursting with photos of a younger Gloria Graves. They assured me her eyes had always been as sharp and arresting as they were in the more recent photograph. I wasn't sure what to make of this oddity, but it struck me as the strangest thing about Gloria Graves, other than the dearth of photographs of her in most of the articles. She seemed like an odd duck, but I wasn't sure I was on the right track. What did a reclusive film star with a fashion line that Papa Razzi was shooting have to do with the explosion of Invincible Man's boat?

Nothing, I thought.

CHAPTER NINE

Before I'd had a chance to sort out my plans for Tuesday, my home phone was ringing. Daisy blinked at it a few times before answering, as if to ask, "who on earth is calling at this time of the morning?" But she didn't seem surprised when she handed the phone over to me. "Jimmy Cooper."

"Hey, Jimmy, news?"

"I've got that warrant on Angelo Fontanelli. Officially speaking, I can't invite you to ride with me. But unofficially speaking, I've got an address you'll want to write down."

I grinned. Jimmy was a good friend who understood that sometimes, unofficial channels might be exactly what were needed to get things done. I scribbled down the address he gave me and said, "What do you know, my hairdresser is in that neighborhood. Wouldn't it be such a coincidence if we ran into each other?"

"Such. See you later, Sarah."

"Going my way?" Daisy asked.

"No, unfortunately." I crossed the living room to the safe where I kept my pistols. "And I should also move quickly if I'm going to be in the right place at the right time."

Before I'd opened the safe, Daisy spoke up again, her voice soft. "You should take your guitar to get it tuned up."

My guitar case, which sat in the living room closet, had never held a musical instrument, but the hard sides and long neck did a fantastic job of protecting my bow and quiver of arrows, the tools of my trade when I had been the Huntsman in Europe.

I paused a moment to consider her suggestion. I had avoided wearing my costume most of the time I'd been in Las Capas, assuring both myself and Daisy it was a part of my life I'd put behind me. I remained in contact with the other superheroes of Las

Capas in the event my services were needed. More often than not, these days, it meant my investigative services.

But if a superhero, known or otherwise, happened to be present when the police arrived at Angelo Fontanelli's lodgings, rather than a PI, it would give both Jimmy and me some plausible deniability.

It would also enrage my father, if word made it back to Cobalt City. He, too, had been assured that my days as Huntsman were over. My brother, Matthew, was the only Huntsman the world needed, in my father's eyes.

Keeping him happy was part of the reason I'd been willing to give up my superheroic activities when I moved across the country. The other reason was I wasn't as young as I'd been when I went to Europe during the War. I was still as good a shot as I'd ever been—better even than Matthew—but there were also running and jumping parts of the job I wasn't as fond of these days.

But at least in my costume, I could wear flat shoes rather than heels. And if I was careful, I might even be able to keep the Huntsman name out of the papers, which would keep my father from knowing I'd been out with my bow and arrows.

I returned the guns to the safe and opened the closet in the spare bedroom, where my costume was tucked deep in the back, behind our heavy coats and sweaters and wool dresses, the sorts of things we rarely needed in Las Capas. I didn't want to wear the full costume out in the daylight hours, since I'd be driving my car to the scene, but I settled for pieces of it—the green and purple tunic and slim-fitting slacks, the flat black shoes, and the hooded mask that covered my hair and most of my face.

Daisy waited for me near the front door with my gloves and the guitar case. "Go get 'em, hero."

~

I parked several blocks away from the address, donned my hood and gloves, and extracted the bow and quiver from the guitar case. The nearby streets were mostly vacant, though I ducked into alleys a few times to avoid the prying eyes of passersby. Though Las Capas was known to be home to many superheroes, it didn't mean we always wanted to make a scene while working.

I made my way nearer to the address Jimmy had given me at street level, then ascended a fire escape on a nearby building to give myself a birds' eye view of the area.

In spite of my last-minute wardrobe change, I'd still arrived before the police. I took some time scoping out the address Jimmy had given me. It was a small three-story brownstone apartment building. By the size of it, I estimated four apartments per floor, and Angelo's address had included a 201. Even without that information, I'd have pegged the left-hand apartment on the front of the building as his—all the other front-facing apartments had windows open, with light curtains fluttering in the breeze. The one that looked to be Angelo's had heavy drapes covering the windows, which were all closed. The place had to be sweltering in the afternoons if he always kept it like that.

Three squad cars pulled up outside the building, and Detective Cooper got out of one of them, one of half a dozen policemen now on the scene. He looked around casually at street level, then scanned the nearby rooftops.

I peeked over the edge of the rooftop just enough so he could see me and nodded. Maybe he wouldn't realize it was me right away, since he'd rarely seen my costume, but he at least would know someone was watching his back. He was smart enough to put two and two together, I thought.

He met my gaze, then looked at the windows I'd been watching and nodded before turning his attention back to me.

I gave him a second quick nod.

With that, he led the rest of the police officers into the building, and I waited, listening for any gunshots or signs of a scuffle. I nocked an arrow that would penetrate and cling to the mortar between the stones and provide me with a rappelling line into the apartment if need be.

Silence followed. The drapes rustled, and Jimmy poked his head between them, catching my eye and shaking his head.

I'd gotten all dressed up for nothing.

I watched as the police returned from their inspection of Angelo's apartment and reentered their cars. Jimmy remained outside of the cars as he spoke to the officer he'd ridden with, tapped the roof of the car, and watched as all three cars drove off, leaving him alone outside the building. He looked up at me, and I jerked my head to the side, indicating the alley I'd meet him in, before descending the fire escape.

"No luck?" I asked as I reached the alley.

"No luck. Looks like he cleared out fast. I'm going to talk to the super, see if she knows anything, but that warrant didn't do us any good." He jerked his chin toward my costume. "So you're dressing up for investigations, now?"

"This seemed a little more discreet than going to a salon nowhere near this neighborhood."

"Huh," he said, narrowing his eyes and sharing a knowing smirk. "The Lady Huntsman, in Las Capas. Who'd have thought?"

I shrugged. "I'm hoping not a lot of folks, honestly. My father would be happier that way. I shouldn't use the Huntsman name, either."

"Then what should I call you?"

"Sarah's fine."

Jimmy shook his head. "You're in costume. I know how this goes. Legally, in costume, your identity is protected. Justice made sure that passed City Council."

He was right, of course. In Las Capas, superheroes had the option to be known by their normal identity or to keep it protected, thanks to General Justice. Since I hadn't been active in costume more than once or twice since I'd arrived on the West Coast, it had never come up for me. But I would need a name, and the sooner the better, just in case someone spotted me returning to my car.

Normally, I'd have brainstormed ideas with Daisy before making a decision, but I blurted out, "Sure Shot."

It was as good a name as any. It emphasized my skills, and it didn't ascribe a gender to my persona.

"Alright, Sure Shot," Jimmy said. His forehead furrowed a bit as he nodded. "That's a good choice. It'll just take a little getting used to."

"This won't be a regular thing," I said, feeling as though I was betraying Daisy by taking on a new superhero identity. "I'm happy with just being a PI, and only wearing this out when it's necessary."

Jimmy nodded, oblivious to my pangs of guilt. "Then I wish you luck that it's only necessary on rare occasions." He paused. "What's next, then? You got any more leads to follow up on?"

"I'm still trying to find the missing Glenn siblings and waiting to hear back from the coroner. I assume no news there?"

"Not yet." He nodded. "That's my next stop, though. I'll call your answering service if I get anything. I think Daisy was a little surprised to hear from me this morning."

"Well, the answering service wouldn't have gotten me here as quickly. But it'll do for a message later. Thanks, Jimmy."

"Anytime, Sure Shot."

~

I swung by the house to change clothes and drop off my bow. My next logical step was to continue pursuing the wayward Glenn siblings, since I could go no further on finding Warren Glenn with Angelo Fontanelli in the wind and no news from the coroner. And the last known location for either remaining Glenn sibling was the Grand Hotel, even if my previous visit had been unproductive.

This time, I dressed more simply and approached the hotel from the alley behind. The front desk clerks would be tight-lipped about the comings and goings of their guests—it was part of the allure of a fancy hotel like the Grand. Other staff, like the maids, were often far more forthcoming with the hotel's dirty laundry, literally and figuratively.

A small group of women clustered outside the back entrance to the hotel, some sharing a cigarette while others pored over a newspaper. Their conversation flowed freely between Spanish and English, and it took me a moment to find the pulse of the mixed language. I'd learned Castilian Spanish as a child, which made the Mexican-flavored Spanish of Las Capas a bit more challenging, but I'd learned enough to use it as an effective means of communication.

I'd picked up a bag of small pastries on my way over, and I presented the bag to the women. "Good morning, need a snack?"

One of the younger women seized the bag gleefully and peered inside, squealing at the contents. Several of the others joined her in her excitement, but one of the older women hung back. "What do you want?" she asked in Spanish.

I gave her an understanding nod. "I'm trying to find someone who was staying in the hotel, but she left. Her name is Clarisse Glenn."

"Glenn?" one of the younger women, her nametag identifying her as Natalie, said. "Warren Glenn's sister?"

The older woman, whose nametag said Louisa, hushed Natalie. "What do you want her for?" she asked me.

I decided to take the honest approach. "She hired me as a private investigator, but I haven't been able to find her since then. I need to ask her some more questions, based on what I've learned so far."

Louisa glanced at the younger women, then back at me. "Break time's almost over."

I nodded. "Is there a better time I could come back? Perhaps buy you a coffee?"

The younger women crammed pastries into their mouths, dabbing at the bits of powdered sugar on each other's faces and straightening their aprons before hurrying inside.

"Break's over for them," Louisa said, once they had departed, leaving the two of us in the alley. "You got cigarettes?"

I didn't smoke often, but I did carry a package of cigarettes, as they came in handy in situations like this. Offering her one, along with a book of matches, I asked, "Do you know how to find Miss Glenn?"

She lit the cigarette, took a drag, and blew out a plume of smoke, then shook her head. "I'm not sure about finding her. I don't think she wants to be found. Her brother, either—at least the one who was staying here."

"Archie," I supplied.

She nodded. "He wasn't here much. A week, maybe? Left his things behind, but he didn't come back, best as I can tell. The sister, she was here longer, but I don't think she slept much."

I frowned. Though the timeframe matched up with when Clarisse had told me Archie had gone missing, if Clarisse had still been in the hotel, why hadn't I been able to contact her? "But she was still around?"

"Some, yes," Louisa said. "Sunday night, I think, she took some of her things and left. No one at all in the room—no, that's not right. No one *staying* in the room after that."

"No one staying?" I arched an eyebrow. "Someone was in the room, though?"

74

Louisa shrugged. "I didn't see anyone, you know. But things were moved around a bit. Like someone was there looking for something."

I nodded. Hotels like the Grand had ways of setting a room to its default, the way they wanted guests to see the room when they arrived. A maid would notice when things were not done in the correct way, particularly if they had extensive experience in the hotel, like Louisa seemed to have. "Is there anything else you can tell me about Clarisse or Archie Glenn?"

Louisa shook her head, but her eyes narrowed. "Maybe. When I arrived on Monday morning, there was a car waiting outside. It was still dark, so I couldn't see the people inside too well, but the profile of the man in the backseat, it looked a lot like Warren Glenn." She shook her head again. "But that couldn't be."

"I understand he and his brother looked quite similar," I said.

At that, Louisa nodded. "But not so alike you couldn't tell the difference. They carry themselves differently, you know?" She stood upright, shoulders thrust back, and a jaunty tilt to her chin. "Warren, much confidence." Then she slumped a bit, almost folding in on herself. "Archie, not so much."

"And the man in the car, the profile?" I asked, my voice soft.

She shrugged, but jutted her chin out. "He had a fine chin."

I pulled the pack of cigarettes from my bag and pressed them and the matches into Louisa's hands. "Thank you, thank you so much for your time."

She smiled and nodded, tucking away the cigarettes. "I hope you find who you need to find."

I hurried away, my mind flying over the possibilities. If Warren and Archie were twins, what were the odds someone mixed them up? What if Archie had taken Warren's boat out on the night it exploded? That could explain the body they'd found.

It still didn't answer the question of where the other Glenn siblings were, but the profile in the darkened car was an intriguing hint. What if Warren had gone into hiding after his boat exploded, perpetuating the rumor that he'd perished, and then retrieved his sister as soon after as he could do so safely?

~

I checked in with my answering service as soon as I reached my office. Catherine was her usual chipper self. "Afternoon, Sarah. I've got a message for you from Danny over at the coroner's office to give a call as soon as you're in."

"Nothing more to the message?"

"'Fraid not."

"Thanks, Catherine. I suspect I'm going to be headed to the First Precinct after I return this call. If there's anything urgent for me in the next few hours, can you reach out to Detective Jimmy Cooper down there?"

"Sure, want to define urgent a little more?"

"Anyone with the surname Glenn, Basil Worthington, and anyone with information about Angelo Fontanelli."

"You got it, boss."

"Thanks, Catherine." I hung up in a hurry and dialed the number for the coroner's office situated in the basement of the First Precinct building.

"Coroner's Office, Dr. Langley." The woman had a broad Midwestern accent, the vowels each a mile wide.

"This is Sarah Castile. I had a message from Danny at the coroner's office?"

"Yeah, that's me. Short for Daniella. Sorry, I guess maybe 'Dani' isn't the best message to leave for someone I've never met, but Detective Cooper said to call you straight away."

"Is this about the Glenn examination?"

The line was silent for a moment, and then she said, "Glenn, yeah. Such as it is."

"That seems cryptic."

"You could say that. Do you have time to swing by?" A note of hesitation tinged her voice. "This is ... complicated."

"I'll be right there."

I was on edge for the entire drive over but managed to stick to the speed limit and obey the rules of the road. Luckily, it was mid-afternoon, and not too many folks were on the road at this time of day.

I headed toward Jimmy's office first, but the officer at the desk shook his head. "He's not in, ma'am."

"Do you know where I might find him?"

"Downstairs, I presume."

"Perfect, that's where I'm headed."

The basement had been built to take advantage of the natural outdoor light, making it much better lit and comfortable feeling than many basements. I followed the hallway to the coroner's office, tucked behind a file storage room that occupied much of the center of the building.

Jimmy was deep in conversation with a woman in her early thirties, broad-shouldered and tanned, looking every bit like a farmer's wife stuffed into her Sunday best, topped off with a white coat. Both of them looked up at the sound of my heels on the linoleum.

Jimmy smiled. "Sarah Castile, may I introduce Dr. Daniella Langley, our new coroner."

I extended my hand and shook the coroner's offered hand.

"Now that we've met, please call me Dani. Dr. Langley is my dad and was my granddad." She shrugged, a bit sheepishly. "And I still can't quite get over the fact that it's me as well."

I nodded, smiling. "It's nice to meet you, Dani. And please, call me Sarah. Now, about the body? Or—"

"Body, just the one found," Dani replied, gesturing toward a sheet-covered body. "Jimmy tells me you've got a strong stomach, but I'm just going to warn you anyway, this isn't pretty."

"I don't mind if you want to show me the body, but it's not necessary if you can tell me whose body it is."

Dani and Jimmy shared a glance before Dani responded. "It's not Warren Glenn."

"I suspect there's something more than just that single statement?"

"We were able to get some dental records from Denver. Seems that Warren Glenn has had perfect teeth his entire life, with no issues. But his brother, Archie Glenn, wasn't so lucky." Dani glanced back toward the body. "On two counts."

I smiled in spite of myself. "Sorry, I know that's not appropriate, but it explains quite a bit." Turning to Jimmy, I said, "I got a tip from a maid at the Grand that someone with Warren Glenn's profile was in a car outside of the hotel the morning Clarisse Glenn checked out."

"So this confirms that, then," Jimmy said, shaking Dani's hand. "Well done, Doc."

"It also explains why Clarisse couldn't find Archie," I said. "No leads on Angelo?"

Jimmy tilted his head to the side and shot a quick glance at Dani. "We should let the doc attend to the rest of her business."

"Of course. Thank you, Dani. It was a pleasure meeting you, and I hope to see you again. I hope I won't become a frequent visitor to your office only because of the implications of such."

Dani chuckled. "You were right, Jimmy, she's a charmer." She took my hand again. "The sentiment is mutual, Sarah."

I waited until we were on the stairs before I leaned toward Jimmy and asked, "Don't want the doc to know we're after Angelo?"

"It's more of an embarrassment," Jimmy admitted. "I didn't get my man this morning. Bad for my reputation."

I paused on the staircase, where we remained out of sight of the main floor of the precinct. "Then we need to find him as soon as we can."

"I don't disagree, but I think we might be better suited for a divide and conquer strategy."

"Oh?"

He shrugged. "I've got the warrant. You're working for Clarisse Glenn, and you've got information she needs to know."

"And not a clue where she is," I said with a sigh.

"No, but I've got a list of addresses waiting on my desk. All known residences of Basil Worthington, which also all happen to be small cottages on the grounds of a home owned by Warren Glenn."

I smiled as I connected what Jimmy was suggesting to what he wasn't saying. Now that I knew I was looking for Warren and not Archie, finding the chauffeur might answer a lot of questions. "Then I'll be off to drive around town, I suppose."

"And I'll get our man, sooner or later."

CHAPTER TEN

I marked the location of Warren Glenn's houses on my map of the Cerulean City area, because they ranged from Las Capas all the way to Rosita Heights. It would be a Herculean task to visit even a handful of them in a single day, and it was already afternoon. So I picked out the nearest one as my starting point.

The house in question was nearly at the top of the hill overlooking the bay, with commanding views of the water, most of Las Capas, and even a few rooms with views into the valley to the east and beyond. Only the northern views were truncated by the house's position on the hillside. The outside bore the pillars common to the Italianate style, though I could confirm the only thing in Italy that looked anything like that was in the ruins of the Roman structures. And as was the way of many things in California, the style married the Italianate to the Spanish, with all of the walls in cream stucco and the ubiquitous red clay tiled roof.

As I pulled down the long driveway and into the circular plaza surrounding an elaborate statuary fountain, a few gardeners looked up from their work. I parked and climbed out of the car, scanning the area for someone to speak with.

A moment passed before an older Mexican man in a tidy suit came to the door. "May I help you, ma'am?" he asked in heavily accented English.

"I'm looking for Miss Clarisse Glenn," I said, then repeated myself in Spanish as I approached, ducking into the shadow of the house and out of the scorching sun. "Do you know where I might find her?"

"No, ma'am, I'm sorry," he said, sticking with English, but averting his gaze.

I pressed the point. "Miss Glenn hired me to help her find her brother, Archibald. I have information I need to share with her."

The man shot a glance over his shoulder, somewhere toward the depths of the house, then looked back at me. "She's not here."

"Has she been?" I asked.

The still expression on his face faltered, and his voice wavered. "Yes, of course, Miss Glenn visited Mr. Glenn. As families do."

My eyes finally adjusted to the dimness of the house's interior, and I could see a few people peeking around corners toward me. All of them wore uniforms of some sort, a veritable army of household staff, all watching our interaction. "I'm sorry to have heard about your employer's accident," I said softly, though loud enough for the other staff to hear.

Again, the man's gaze slid away from mine, and he bit at his lip. I followed his gaze, which went to a telephone nook near the front door. I had a sneaking suspicion that as soon as my car pulled away from the house, he would be making a phone call, and I wished I had a way to hear that conversation. He knew something he wasn't letting on, and though he was maintaining his façade better than some people I had questioned, I could see his tells and the cracks that were developing.

I stretched out on the farthest limb I could, whispering in rapid-fire Spanish. "I'm here to help Invincible Man."

The man's eyebrows flew up and he shook his head. "No, no, no," he mumbled rapidly before straightening. "I'm afraid I don't understand."

I set my lips in a firm line and handed him a business card. "If Miss Glenn comes by, please ask her to call the number on the card."

He looked at the card, and I took a moment to tap the line proclaiming me as a "Private Investigator" with my fingernail. "Please, let me help," I whispered in Spanish.

"Thank you, ma'am. I will pass this on to Miss Glenn for you."

"Thank you." Turning away, I returned to my car slowly, taking in the few staff I could see nearby. They were going through the motions of working, but only so much as they needed to do to maintain the estate. They were not preparing to close an unused or unneeded house. They were operating as though this was business as usual. And it was, since Warren Glenn hadn't been killed in the explosion. But if I could recognize this, who else might see their behavior and wonder? Who else might come to the same conclusion as me?

As I pulled out of the driveway, I worried that I'd found my answer, as a pair of black sedans approached. I slowed and watched them in my rearview mirror. If it was the police, I'd continue on my way. But if it was anyone else ...

The man in the back seat in the second car, seated behind the driver, was a heavy I'd seen at Papa Razzi's house.

I turned sharply at the next intersection, parking my car just past the end of the street. There wasn't time to put my costume on, even if I had it with me. But I had a pair of flat-heeled shoes and a black raincoat in the trunk, for emergencies. And Daisy, bless her, had tucked a masked cowl into the glovebox, for situations just like this one. I would look ridiculous if anyone spotted me, but the idea was to not be spotted.

I vaulted the low stone wall separating Warren's house from that of his nearest neighbor and picked through the tall hedges running along the property line. I heard raised voices that kept me headed toward the house in spite of the foliage.

"C'mon, Pedro. We know your boss had a payment waiting for us," one of the enforcers said, glaring at the man I had spoken with previously.

"No, no, sir," he said, shaking his head and holding his hands in front of him, emphasizing his answer.

"Well, you won't mind if we take a look around, see if there's anything worth taking as payment? Or anything else of interest?"

I didn't like the direction this was headed. Warren's staff had numbers, but they wouldn't stand up to mob enforcers. And I had a pistol, which would not be enough to stop eight armed men, or even to drive them away. If I had my bow, I would have had a chance. But I hadn't thought I'd need it twice in one day.

I didn't have any way to request backup, either, without driving to find the nearest payphone. By that point, these mobsters wouldn't still be around, and the likelihood was that some of Warren's staff might be injured. At that point, I'd be better off calling for an ambulance rather than reinforcements.

Before I had to make the choice to charge in on my own with my pistol, a low thrumming sound resonated across the yard, followed by a brilliant flash of blue-white light. I ducked and covered my face, not sure what had just happened. A crackling sound followed, and I peeked to see a shimmering wall of the same blue-white light between where Pedro had been standing a moment ago and the mobsters, who looked as confused as I felt.

This was new. This wasn't something I'd seen General Justice's tech do, nor something Invincible Man could do. I ran through the list of other heroes in Las Capas, and still came up blank. There wasn't enough lightning for this to be Ciclón, and it wasn't tinted an unnatural green, so it seemed unlikely to be something Rashimi had conjured up. And Pícaro was like me—she had training and skill, but no powers that I knew of.

"Stand back," a voice boomed, artificial and tinny like it was emanating from a speaker at a drive-in movie.

I squinted against the light. I knew General Justice was working with robotics, but I couldn't make out enough details to be sure that this was one of his.

The light shifted as it pressed toward the mobsters, all of whom were now scrambling toward their cars.

"The old lady ain't gonna like this," one of them squealed.

"Shut up and drive," another replied.

As the cars started and sped away, the shimmering wall followed them. But my eyes were glued to the being who seemed to be in control of the wall as the obscuring light faded with distance. They stood more than twelve feet tall and possessed human-like appendages, but the arms, legs, and head appeared to be constructed of welded steel drums, surrounding a torso that might have once been the passenger compartment of a car. They moved more fluidly than I would have anticipated something that bulky to be able to move, and the head rotated back and forth, revealing a portion of the steel drum of the head that had been removed and replaced with some sort of glass plate. But behind the plate was more of the same glowing blue-white.

"Someone is in the bushes," the voice intoned, the glass plate turned in my direction.

I rose immediately, gun tucked away and hands up. "I was making sure those mob enforcers weren't going to hurt anyone here."

Pedro squinted in my direction, and I pulled off my masked cowl. "Ah, this young lady was here earlier asking after Master Glenn and his sister."

"What is your intention?" the steel-drum figure asked.

"I have information for Miss Glenn," I said, then crossed my arms over my chest. "What is *your* intention? And who are you?"

"You may call me Polonium. I am here to protect those who have not been gifted with powers."

"Ah, so you're new," I murmured. My gaze flickered toward Pedro. Was this who Pedro had called? Or had he called Warren, or General Justice, who then sent in the nearest superhero? Or did they even know about this Polonium? I'd have to check in with General Justice later.

The voice continued. "And your name?"

I hesitated for a moment, unsure how to introduce myself to someone else who seemed to be a superhero. I'd been wearing my makeshift mask, but I hadn't established myself with the other superheroes in the city as Sure Shot, so I'd be as much of a wild card as Polonium. If I called myself Huntsman now, all of Warren's staff would hear, or at least learn about it later. That increased the odds of word getting back to my father.

So I opted for the answer that wouldn't out me in that regard. "Sarah Castile. I'm a private investigator who happened to be in the neighborhood." I held up the mask. "This was just to protect myself, as I'm not interested in the mob hunting me down."

While I was fascinated by this hero and their name, I didn't have time to stand around now that introductions were out of the way. My lack of costume and a stated superhero identity, too, meant I didn't have a good reason to dig deeper at the moment. And I had other places to be. "Thank you for protecting those who aren't gifted with powers." I turned my attention back toward Pedro. "Please do have Miss Glenn call me, and I won't take up any more of your time."

~

The last thing I expected as I was driving toward the next of Warren Glenn's houses was another explosion.

Yet again, it wasn't directed at me, but yet again, it was far too close for comfort. I parked my car and sat for a moment, calming myself before I got out and ran toward the location.

It had been a few blocks over from where I was driving, so it took me a few minutes to find the right block. Already the sirens were nearby, and a crowd of onlookers clued me in to the source—

what remained of an unidentifiable car was burning at the edge of a minor street.

I started to turn away from the scene—what were the odds this had anything to do with my case? But a pair of squad cars screeched to a halt and Jimmy leapt out of one of them.

"Sarah, are you alright?"

I nodded. "I just happened to be a couple of blocks away, but—"

"It's Angelo Fontanelli's car," Jimmy said, his words in a rush.

"Really?" I turned back toward the car. The fire trucks had arrived and were battling the blaze, so all I could see was smoke and steam. "How can you tell?"

"We had a tip called in that his car had been spotted, so we were en route when the explosion happened." Jimmy shrugged. "Not going to have anything for sure until the fire's out, but the tip gave us the plates."

I squinted at the tail end of the car, trying to make out any of the license plate, but still couldn't see the details of the car. Giving up on that, I moved closer to Jimmy. "Even if it was his car, that doesn't find him."

Jimmy nodded and answered me in a quiet voice. "We've got a bunch of plainclothes in the area, watching who's coming and going. If he was parked here because he's in the neighborhood, and he tries to make a run for it, we might just find him. What do you say to Sure Shot taking to a rooftop for backup?"

I looked around to see if anyone was looking my way and then headed back toward my car. I was still wearing my flat-soled shoes and raincoat, and my cowled mask was in my purse. What I didn't have with me was my bow.

But tucked deep into my purse, I did have a small box of specialized points for my arrows. They worked better when fired, as the speed helped trigger them. General Justice had put this set together for me as a thank you for helping him out with some investigative work, and I'd modified them to work, in a pinch, as grenades with a pressure-sensitive alternate means of deployment. I could press the button and drop them from the top of a building, and they'd work just as well as they would if fired. I fished out the smoke screen, the concussive blast, and the flare and put away the rest.

Now if I spotted Angelo Fontanelli, I'd be ready to slow him down and draw the police toward him.

CHAPTER ELEVEN

From the rooftop I'd selected, I had a good view of the situation near the burning car. The fire department had doused the flames but were still keeping a wide perimeter as the smoke and steam slowly dissipated. Most of the spectators had wandered off now that there wasn't a burning car to gawk at. The few people still near the car were Jimmy and the officer who had ridden with him, now in conversation with the fire chief, and a handful of other men and women who seemed to be keeping an eye out for Angelo Fontanelli.

I had the best view of the street from one corner in particular, so I ensconced myself there. My attention was drawn to a fluttering scrap of white paper wedged between two of the bricks in the parapet at this corner, and I grabbed at it to remove the distraction.

My fingers brushed against the paper, and the tactile sensation flashed me back to my time in Europe. It wasn't just a scrap of paper, it was a cigarette paper. But the texture was creamy, incredibly smooth. This wasn't the sort of cigarette paper that most people used, in Europe or America. This was high end.

I looked more closely at the paper. It was whole, folded in such a way that indicated someone had placed it in between the bricks, as though they intended to use it soon.

There was a faint smudge of ash atop the parapet, as though someone had been smoking here. They'd tried to wipe away the evidence, but there was still just enough there for me to catch a faint whiff of the burned tobacco, and that, too, sent me back to Europe.

I'd spent two weeks in Florence with The Venetian on the trail of a contract killer. We had always been one step behind him, and eventually he vanished, moving on to somewhere where he wasn't being hunted by an American archer and an Italian vampire turned do-gooder. But he'd left behind this same sort of cigarette paper, and ashes that smelled identical to these. What were the odds?

I scanned the space for any additional clues. Tucked into a deeper crevice than the cigarette paper had been, I found another slip of paper, this one far more common, but with an address scrawled in a spidery handwriting. I hadn't noted the address of the building before I'd gone up the fire escape, but the street name was the one we were on, and the number was likely this building. I didn't recognize the handwriting, but I tucked the paper into my pocket nonetheless.

As I did, I caught another scent that made my stomach plummet. This paper bore the unmistakable smell of that assassin's aftershave.

And all the pieces clicked together.

Yiorgos "The Greek" Nikolaides. Graduate of the fabled Factory, a training program for contract killers that no one had ever been able to locate. His death count in Florence alone was near a dozen, and he'd been there two or three weeks.

He fit the description Bob had given me at the marina. Tall, slender, dark haired. Expensive Italian leather shoes. I hadn't gone into the marina, and I don't know if the scent of his tobacco and aftershave would have lingered there like they did here.

His weapon of choice?

Remote detonated explosives.

The sort that could be triggered from here to target a car on the street below, when the moment was right.

Which probably meant Angelo Fontanelli wasn't our killer, and he wasn't available for questioning, either.

~

Back down at street level, I approached Jimmy, my hooded mask tucked back into my purse and my makeshift grenades returned to their box. "I've got a lead."

He tilted his head to the side. "On the roof?"

I handed him the cigarette paper and the note with the address on it, which I confirmed was the building the car was parked outside. "They won't mean much to you, but that cigarette paper is high end, Italian. There's an aftershave scent on the address slip. And there was some remnant ash of a specific kind of tobacco."

"She's a modern day Sherlock Holmes," the officer beside him said with a chuckle.

I favored him with a quick smile. "We're looking for a contract killer. Yiorgos Nikolaides, also known as 'The Greek.' He's known for using explosives, remotely detonated." I glanced at the car. "I think we're going to find Angelo's remains in that car."

Jimmy nodded quickly. "We haven't been able to get in there yet, but yeah, there was someone in the driver's seat when it went up." He paused, pursing his lips. "But contract killer? I suppose that makes sense for an attempt on Warren Glenn, but why Angelo?"

I shook my head. "Haven't sorted that out yet. But the answer might be tied to who hired a contract killer, and why? The Greek is an expensive choice, from my understanding. Last time I encountered him, he was working for a family with ties to the Borgias."

"*The* Borgias?" the other officer scoffed. "They're still around?"

I nodded. "Europe's full of old families, especially the ones with a lot of money."

"Okay, so someone with money, who wanted both Warren Glenn and Angelo Fontanelli out of the picture." Jimmy paused, stroking his chin. "Razzi, you think?"

"What's the motive on Angelo?" I asked. "Or Warren, for that matter?"

Jimmy shook his head. "Yeah, I don't know. Where else are Angelo Fontanelli and Warren Glenn connected?"

"I guess that's what I have to figure out next."

Another police officer approached us, holding a battered paperback in his hand. "Detective Cooper, we found the room Angelo was renting here, but it's pretty Spartan. This was the only thing we found."

I tilted my head to the side to look at the title and was surprised to see it wasn't a novel, but rather a biography of Vera Lancaster. "Well that's odd," I murmured.

"What's that?" Jimmy asked.

"Vera Lancaster. Warren Glenn's chauffeur worked for her in London, but she died eighteen years ago. It's just an odd coincidence, I think."

Jimmy nodded. "Maybe, maybe not. Angelo doesn't strike me as the silent film star kind of guy." He took the book from the other officer and handed it to me. "In case there's some sort of connection."

I nodded as I accepted the book, but my mind was already miles away. Was this the connection between Angelo Fontanelli and Warren Glenn? How could a decades-dead silent film star be the link between a pair of otherwise unrelated murders?

Daisy was going to want to kill me, but it was time for me to start mapping this out in the study.

~

Daisy was already home when I arrived, warming up a can of tomato soup on the stove. "Well, now that you're here, I suppose we'd better turn this into a meal."

I nodded, though my thoughts were still distant. I felt like I was close to piecing everything together, but something was still missing.

"Uh-oh," Daisy said. "I know that look. Get the cheese out of the fridge. You're going to butter some bread for grilled cheese and talk me through this case until it clicks. Let's go."

"Alright, but I need to make a quick phone call first," I said. I ducked into the study and dialed General Justice's number.

His wife, Donna, answered. "Justice residence."

"Hi, Donna, it's Sarah Castile, calling for Richard."

"Oh, hi, Sarah! So good to hear from you! Unfortunately, Richard's not home right now. Do you want me to pass a message on to him?"

I hesitated. Donna Justice wasn't a superhero, but because her husband was, she knew a lot of the bigger players in Las Capas. What were the odds she'd already know about Polonium? I shrugged. It was worth a shot. "I don't suppose you've heard anything through Richard about a new individual patrolling the city?"

"Oddly enough, that's what he's checking out. Possibly a rogue robot?"

"Could be," I replied, thinking over my encounter with Polonium. There had been no indication they were human, and I had thought the suit looked a bit like some of General Justice's gear. Could someone other than General Justice have perfected an unmanned flying suit? "When he gets back in, could you ask him to give me a call? If it's not too late, of course."

"Of course, Sarah. While I've got you on the phone, what is it going to take to get you and Daisy over here for dinner?"

I demurred politely, but my mind was already working through the bits of the case Daisy knew about, and where I'd need to start to catch her up on where I was now. I gave non-committal answers to Donna's questions, finally ending our call with an excuse of helping Daisy out with dinner, as I'd promised I would.

With my mind swirling over the case, I walked back into the kitchen and announced the information Daisy didn't know that would become relevant to our hashing out of the case. "Warren Glenn's alive—"

Daisy interrupted. "He's what?"

I shrugged. "I have reason to believe he's fine, but in hiding. Because that's not the half of it. His brother Archie is dead instead, and so is Angelo Fontanelli. And I know who killed them."

"Then why the creased forehead, darling? You've got this solved, right?"

"No, I still don't know why. The murderer is a contract killer who goes by the name of The Greek, so I still have to figure out who's behind the contract. Who would have wanted a prominent actor and a low-level mob enforcer dead?"

"Someone who doesn't like dark-haired men?" Daisy joked. "Gosh, I don't know. Warren owed the mob, but that was paid off, right?"

"Maybe, maybe not," I said. "I was canvassing one of Warren Glenn's properties, and some mob goons showed up at demanding payment from his staff there. Though now that I know Warren's alive, I wonder if the Fontanellis know too, and they were demanding money to keep their silence?"

Daisy shook her head. "But that wouldn't explain Angelo being killed, would it?"

I frowned. "You're right, it doesn't. All Angelo's done is spill the beans to Jimmy and me that the boat had been retrieved, while we were talking to Papa Razzi. Assuming Angelo was yelling about that because the mob hired The Greek, then maybe someone decided Angelo was a loose cannon and he needed to be taken out too. But the other thing I don't understand is why the mob would need to outsource? They have plenty of assassins they wouldn't have to pay to do the work."

"Maybe The Greek has special techniques?"

I nodded, handing Daisy the sloppily buttered bread. "The Greek works in explosives. Which is effective, unless you get the wrong guy."

"And you're certain it was Warren who was the target, not his brother?"

"No, I suppose not." I considered that possibility to the scents of bread crisping to golden brown and cheese melting. "Okay, I don't know enough about Archie to make this work." I shook my head. "I think we have to assume Warren was the target."

Daisy slid our sandwiches onto plates and ladled the soup into bowls, and we sat down to eat and continue considering the case.

"Oh, before I forget, I want you to know that I'm not getting back into the superhero life, but I did come up with a new name."

Daisy looked at me over the spoonful of soup she was bringing to her lips. "Well, that's a whole lot of pre-explaining just to tell me a new name."

"I promised you when we moved in together that I wouldn't go back to a life of patrolling and being out odd hours," I said, reaching a hand across the table to her.

She took my hand, squeezed it, and smiled. "I appreciate that, Sarah. But I also know you've got fighting crime in your blood, literally. It makes sense that now and again, you'll need to break out the bow and a secret identity. To help with your legitimate investigations, if nothing else." She paused. "So, what's the name?"

I took a deep breath. "Sure Shot."

"Sure Shot," she repeated, then nodded and smiled. "Oh, that's good. Well chosen."

"You really think so?" I asked.

"Absolutely. I don't think I could have done better."

I smiled. "I'm sure you could have, but hearing you say that is a relief. Alright, back to the case then. Where were we?"

"How publicly known is it that the killer got Archie instead of Warren?" she asked.

"It's not, as far as I know. I was trying to find Warren earlier, before the second explosion, in fact." I filled her in on what I saw at his house, including the appearance of the new superhero, Polonium, while we ate.

"Boy, this is a whole big mess." Daisy paused and narrowed her eyes at me. "I suppose this means you're going to web up the wall of the study again?"

"Better there than the living room, right?"

She sighed dramatically, but a smile flickered on her lips the whole time. "I suppose, darling. Just try to not stay up too late working?"

CHAPTER TWELVE

In spite of Daisy's admonition to not stay up too late, it was past midnight when I stumbled to bed. Once there, I tossed and turned for what seemed like hours, and I was groggy when the alarm went off on Wednesday morning, feeling as though I'd spent the whole night rehashing the case.

I was still at a loss, even with laying everything out visually. I couldn't find a strong connection between Warren and Angelo, no matter how I looked at it. And I couldn't figure out how The Greek might play into the whole thing, either. Someone had hired him, but none of the possible suspects seemed to be in a position to have done so. Which meant it was time for me to start researching the finances of some of the suspects.

A visit to the financial district meant a whole different wardrobe and purse selection than the one I'd been carrying, so I worked on transferring necessary things to my nicer purse while Daisy served up breakfast. She may have complimented my dinner cooking skills, but she made the better breakfasts between the two of us.

She glanced at the detritus of my rearranging when she brought my plate to me. "Oh, you got a biography of Vera Lancaster?"

"It belonged to Angelo Fontanelli—or at least the police found it in the room he was renting before ... well, before his car exploded."

She returned to the stove for her plate, then picked up the book to page through it while she ate. "You know, it's always been the oddest thing to me, how interchangeable a lot of early movie stars were."

"What do you mean?"

"Someone somewhere would pick a look, and then everyone else emulated it." She set the book down between us, opened to a photograph of who I presumed was Vera Lancaster. "See, Vera was the style maker of her day. Then everyone wanted to look like her."

I looked at the photograph more closely, frowning when I reached Vera's eyes. "May I?" I asked, reaching for the book.

Daisy relinquished it, and I turned it around, looking at the photo of Vera Lancaster upright. I could see what Daisy meant, in that many of the women of that era had similar hairstyles, and they all wore their makeup in similar palettes. But there was a dramatic similarity between Vera Lancaster and Gloria Graves, especially looking at Vera Lancaster's eyes.

I flipped a few pages farther in the book and found a photograph that looked nearly identical to the one I'd seen in the newspaper. The one of Gloria Graves. According to this book, however, this was Vera Lancaster in 1908.

I set the book down in front of Daisy, and she frowned. "That's not Vera ... well there you go, just like I was saying. Gloria Graves looked just like Vera Lancaster in her heyday."

"I'm not sure if that's it," I said slowly, the pieces clicking together. "I found a photograph almost identical to this one in the newspaper, but it was Gloria Graves."

"You think they're the same person?" Daisy asked, her eyebrows shooting upward.

"I know it's far-fetched, but bear with me. Some people have powers of incredible strength or speed. What about incredible longevity? Remaining eternally young?"

"That would be amazing!" Daisy exclaimed.

"Unless you're in the public eye. People would start to notice if you never aged."

"Sure, but like you said, there are all sorts of people with powers."

"And how many of them maintain two separate identities—one normal human being, and one superhero?" I chuckled, counting myself among those with two identities.

Daisy nodded. "But I'm not sure why an actress would be among those."

She didn't know what I knew about Warren Glenn, and I wasn't about to give away his secret, especially now that I knew he was alive. "There are all sorts of reasons why people keep their professional and private lives separate." I paused, my thoughts catching up to the conclusion we'd just reached. "Basil Worthington worked for Vera Lancaster."

"That's what you've said, yes."

"Do you realize what that means?"

Daisy's eyes widened. "That he'd be able to come to the same conclusion. That it would be obvious to him if Vera Lancaster and Gloria Graves are one and the same."

I nodded. "And if Angelo had this book around, I wonder if he'd arrived at that point. What if Warren wasn't The Greek's target? What if it was Basil?"

"Because Vera-slash-Gloria doesn't want her secret identity getting out."

"Exactly. So she hires The Greek to ensure secrecy can be maintained." I sighed. "It's a strong theory at this point, but not enough to go to the police yet. I need to do some more work on this, but at least I feel like I've got a better sense of direction now."

"I can do some more digging too, if you like. You said Percy knew Vera Lancaster?"

I shook my head. "He did, but I need you to be extra careful. If we're right, we don't want anyone catching wind of the direction this is taking. The Greek is dangerous, and I don't want either of us to wind up on his hit list. We need to keep this quiet for now."

~

I spent my morning visiting some of Warren Glenn's other homes, but the staff at each of them was no more help than they'd been at the first house I'd visited. At least these houses had fewer instances of mobsters and superheroes I'd never met. But they also had gotten me no closer to finding Warren or Clarisse.

I began to wonder if it was worth my time to keep looking for the remaining Glenns. They were likely laying low, which was safer for everyone involved, including themselves and Basil. I would be better off turning my attention to getting the information I needed to prove The Greek was behind the explosions and he'd been hired by Gloria Graves.

I dialed General Justice's house again, hoping to catch him at home.

"Justice residence, Richard speaking,"

"Richard, it's Sarah Castile."

"Sarah, good to hear from you. Sorry I didn't get back to you last night, but I didn't make it home until after it seemed appropriate to call you back."

"Did you track down the new patroller?" I asked.

"I did, and based on what Donna told me when she mentioned you called, I think you may have been the first of us to encounter him."

"Can you tell me anything more about him?"

"Despite initial appearances, the suit is manned. The size is due to the amount of shielding necessary to keep the power source protected and the hero's identity concealed."

I sighed. "And did you discover the hero's identity?"

Richard chuckled. "Turns out I already knew him. And it seems you do too. He told me to give his regards to Sarah, from, and I quote, 'an old Yorkie'."

"Percy?" I exclaimed, then chuckled along with Richard as he responded to my outburst. "Well, that sly old dog. Do you know why he showed up at Warren Glenn's house right after the mob arrived yesterday?"

"He said he'd been following the mobsters to see what they were up to and saw a place where he could do some good."

"His appearance certainly did," I said. "Well, then I suppose I feel a bit better about Daisy being on set, knowing he'll be keeping an eye out for her."

"Mmm, yes," Richard said. He quickly changed the subject. "So, anything new on your end of the case?"

"Yes, unfortunately. Ever heard of The Greek?"

"The Factory graduate?"

"One and the same. I believe he's responsible for—" I trailed off. I had no idea whether General Justice knew Warren was alive, and I felt like this was the sort of information that shouldn't be bandied about too freely. "There's been a second explosion now. Remotely detonated, as far as I can tell. I found The Greek's brand of cigarette paper and tobacco ash at the scene, and I suspect if anyone had checked buildings with a nice line of sight of the marina on the night of the boat explosion, they'd have found more of the same."

"Do you suspect he's got more work in the city?"

"Maybe," I admitted.

"Who do you think he'll come after next?" General Justice asked.

"The likely answer would be Basil Worthington. Looking at the big picture, there's a good chance he was the target all along. There was one body recovered from the boat explosion, so if The Greek has any information sources in the city, he'll know it wasn't Basil's body. The fact that he stuck around afterward makes me think he may know things didn't go as planned. Unless he started out with a longer hit list than just Basil."

"But we can't find Basil, either."

"If he's in hiding, perhaps with Clarisse Glenn, they may be safe. I can't track her down, and she hired me for this case."

"I'm not so sure they're safe. You would think we'd have heard something if they were."

"Maybe. But if they were to contact us, that might give The Greek all the information he needs to find them." I shook my head, knowing my reassurances wouldn't help any when it came to General Justice. "If you've got a safe way to find and contact them, I'm not going to stop you. Just be cautious about it."

"What about you? What's your next move?"

"Still working on that," I said. It was an honest answer. I didn't want to track down The Greek directly, and I anticipated that if Gloria Graves was behind this mess, she'd be well protected. I needed an in of some sort, and I didn't see anything presenting itself.

"Say, did you know Gloria Graves is having a party this evening, launching some new fashion line she's developed?"

I arched an eyebrow. "I did not. How did you get wind of that?"

"The missus. It's a big high society to-do. Fortunately, we have other plans."

"Well, I don't," I said. "I may have to see if I can't finagle my way into an invite."

"Oh, it's ticketed, actually. Why don't you just take ours? You could say you're my cousin, perhaps?"

I noted he didn't suggest taking Daisy with me, but I had to assume the tickets were for two, and I couldn't imagine finding anyone else to accompany me at the last minute. Daisy, on the other hand, would be ready to go in an instant as soon as I told her about the party. "That's kind of you. When shall I swing by to get the tickets?"

~

I wasn't thrilled about having to dress up in a slinky dress and stiletto heels for the party, but Daisy insisted I had to look like I belonged there if I was going undercover. At least the dress she picked out for me had a loose enough skirt that I could wear my thigh holster and carry a pistol unnoticed.

And she was right about us blending in with the crowd. If anything, my dress wasn't half as glitzy as some of the other attire being worn. I would have stuck out like a sore thumb in the pantsuit I wanted to wear.

Despite it being a ticketed event, the venue, a movie theatre in the heart of Las Capas, was packed to the gills. Daisy and I made our way through the lobby, her waving and shouting to some of her industry friends while I focused on getting us into the theatre proper.

The press of humanity was a little lighter once we made it out of the lobby. The theatre was blinding in vivid crimson and gold, but the din was less strident. I scanned the crowd, and my gaze landed on a throne that matched the theatre colors placed right in front of the small stage below the screen. Seated on that throne was a woman who could be none other than Gloria Graves, looking just as young and fresh-faced as she had as Vera Lancaster in her prime. Seeing her with my own eyes confirmed my suspicions—she didn't age—though I had no way of knowing whether that was a byproduct of magic, medical enhancement, or genetics.

I kept my gaze roving, though, trying to locate The Greek. If I didn't see him, that didn't mean he wasn't here, and perhaps even made me more sure he'd be lurking in the wings somewhere.

"I've got to speak with some people," Daisy murmured. "Will you be alright on your own?"

I chuckled softly but nodded. "I may well just go find our seats and wait for you there, but yes, I can manage by myself."

She gave me a gentle peck on the cheek and moved into the press of other people.

"Miss Castile," a voice said slightly behind me.

I looked in that direction and spotted Papa Razzi. Bracing myself, I turned on my most winning smile. "Mister Razzi."

"I think perhaps we got off on the wrong foot the other day. You didn't let Detective Cooper introduce you to me in a proper fashion."

"My apologies," I said. "I find in my line of work that people tend to clam up when they realize they're talking to a private investigator, whether they have anything to hide or not."

He spread his hands in front of him and shrugged. "PIs do have a certain reputation, after all." He gestured with a finger toward someone behind me, and I tensed. "Champagne?"

"Yes, thank you."

Reaching past my shoulder, he retrieved two flutes of champagne from a silver tray and handed me one. "A toast to greater transparency, eh?"

"Greater transparency," I repeated, clinking my glass against his. "I did want to wish you my condolences, Mister Razzi. On Angelo."

Papa Razzi sighed. "Gratzi."

"Prego," I replied, out of habit.

Switching to Italian, he asked, "Oh, you speak the mother tongue?"

I nodded. "I spent some time there after the War."

"Ah, yes. Your accent is Venetian."

Forcing myself not to laugh at how quickly he'd picked up the source of most of my tutoring in Italian, I nodded again. "I understand you've been doing some work with Miss Graves on the line she's debuting tonight. Anything exciting I should know about?"

He shrugged. "You don't strike me as the type who cares about fashion."

"My roommate is far more interested than I am, it's true. But what I'd really like to know more about is Miss Graves. I've heard a rumor she's got a younger man in her web at the moment."

Papa Razzi chuckled. "Miss Graves always has a flock of younger men in her web, Miss Castile."

"What about the Mediterranean looking one?" I asked, craning my neck to scan the crowd again. "Is he one of them?"

"The Gree—" he began, then pressed his lips together. "No, the Mediterranean one isn't one of her hangers on, I don't believe."

He'd already given away too much, though. "So you know The Greek too?"

His gaze darted away from mine. "It was a pleasure getting to know you better, Miss Castile. I should find my date, and my seat."

"Oh, yes, of course," I said. "I should do the same."

I hesitated a moment longer where I was standing. Papa Razzi had confirmed The Greek was in play and involved with Gloria Graves, which was fantastic news for my case. But that didn't put me any closer to finding him, and this didn't seem like the sort of event that would get me in a position to talk to Gloria Graves, either.

I reached into my purse to find the tickets, to determine where Daisy and I would be sitting, but my attention was instead drawn to a small capsule that rolled between my feet and burst into a cloud of acrid smoke, filling my nostrils and lungs as I drew a breath.

Before I could move, though, I was overcome with darkness.

CHAPTER THIRTEEN

Waking up in a bed I didn't recognize was not a good start to my morning. It took me a moment to piece together what had happened. The capsule, the smoke, and the darkness all came rushing back, and I sat up suddenly. My blood pounded in my ears, and black spots danced across my vision, but I tried to ignore them. I didn't understand why, but The Greek must have kidnapped me. I had to get out of here.

I was still in my fancy dress, my heels on the floor beside the bed. A glass of water and bottle of aspirin sat on the table beside the bed, and the curtains were pulled back on the window, which looked out at an enormous and familiar looking palm tree. I blinked a few times, trying to make sense of all of these pieces.

I sniffed at the water and took a tentative sip. It didn't taste unusual, but there were many things that could be put into water to harm a person that would be undetectable by smell. But if The Greek hadn't already killed me, he had a reason for keeping me alive. And the aspirin was calling my name as my head continued to pound, so I shook a pair into my hand and swallowed them with another sip of water.

The tree looming in front of me finally clicked into place. I'd seen that tree at one of Warren Glenn's houses—from a different angle, since I'd been outside. There was a pattern of scars about midway up the trunk I remembered seeing, not the sort I'd seen on other palm trees.

What on earth was I doing at one of Warren Glenn's houses?

Panic set in again as I wondered if The Greek had brought me here because he knew it would be unoccupied. But I still couldn't fathom why he would have kidnapped me. If he'd recognized me as his former rival, why wouldn't he have just killed me outright?

I gave the room a quick once-over, still perched on the edge of the bed. My purse was on a small mirrored dressing table, and my thigh holster and pistol sat beside it. This made even less sense. If The Greek had kidnapped me, he would have taken my pistol, not left it in plain sight.

I slid out of bed, leaving my heels where they sat, and padded over to the dressing table. I flipped open the chamber and confirmed the gun was still loaded with my bullets, not blanks. My purse still had its contents, including the tickets for the fashion show I'd been looking for before I passed out.

I padded to the door and tried the knob, which rotated freely. So I had my weapon, still loaded, and I wasn't locked in this room.

Things were not adding up.

I opened the door slowly, nosing my gun out as I did.

"Sarah?" a voice called. A woman's voice, but it wasn't Daisy.

I peeked out the doorway and came face to face with Clarisse Glenn.

Glancing around frantically, I grabbed her and pulled her into the room, closing the door behind her. "What are you doing here? Are you alright?"

"Sarah, I'm fine. It's okay. You're fine."

"Why are we in your brother's house? Where's The Greek?"

She shook her head, eyes wide. "Oh, God, no, The Greek's not here. Warren and Basil got you out of the party after the capsule went off, before The Greek could get to you."

"What was in the capsule?"

"The Greek tried to knock you out. My brother and Basil were both working the party in disguise. When they realized what was going on, they managed to grab you and leave."

"Where's Daisy?"

"Daisy?" Clarisse asked, cocking her head to the side.

"Clarie?" a voice came from the hallway. "Where'd you go?"

Clarisse opened the door. "I'm in here with Sarah."

"Daisy's my girlfriend," I said. "Where is she?"

Warren stepped into view. "Morning, Sarah. Sorry about the—" He waved his hand vaguely. "All this. What's this about Daisy?"

"Where is she?" I asked again, my voice shaking.

Warren shrugged. "Was she at the party?"

"Yes!" I exclaimed. "Do you have a phone?"

"Yes, sure, come with me," Warren said.

I followed him into a sitting room where Basil was reading the paper. Beside him, a phone sat on an end table, and I ran toward it. Scooping up the receiver, I dialed the number for our house with a shaky hand.

The phone rang. Five, six, seven rings, and no answer.

"Sarah?" Warren asked behind me.

"She's not picking up."

"Call Richard."

I nodded, but my fingers slipped as I tried to hang up the phone to dial General Justice's number.

Gently, Basil took the phone from me and placed it on the receiver, then led me to a chair. I didn't realize how much I was shaking until he had me seated. "Do you want some gin, coffee, tea? Some breakfast? What works best for you?"

"Coffee," I murmured. My brain was still frantic. "Toast."

Basil hurried out of the room, leaving a worried Warren and Clarisse both looking at me.

"It's Thursday," Warren said as he picked up the phone. "Would she have gone to work?"

"If I didn't come home? Probably not."

He dialed swiftly. "Richard. Did The Greek have anyone with him when you spotted him?" He paused. "We don't know where Daisy Dean is." Another pause. "Thanks, Richard." Turning to me, he said, "The Greek didn't have her when he fled the scene. There was a lot of panic over the smoke, Sarah. We almost lost track of you, and we couldn't get our hands on The Greek."

I finally regained enough sense to look up at Warren with a glare. "How long have you known The Greek was involved?" I turned my glare on Clarisse. "And why did you keep avoiding my calls?"

"One thing at a time," Warren said, just as Basil returned with a cup of coffee, pot of cream, and bowl of sugar.

I picked up the coffee and took a long sip, ignoring the heat, willing myself to calm down. But my breathing was still erratic, and my nerves on edge.

"We realized it was The Greek after Angelo was killed," Warren began. "That's also when I reached out to Richard, to clue him in on what was going on. He wasn't sure whether we should tell you or not, given your history with The Greek."

I glared at Warren. "Really? You decided that because I might be an irrational woman about my old rival, you wouldn't tell me he was a threat to my safety and that of my girlfriend?"

"That's not it at all, Sarah," Warren said, his gaze pleading with me. "We were trying to protect you."

"Not telling me things doesn't help me, Warren. I can take care of myself, if I have all of the information."

Clarisse cleared her throat softly. "As for me, I'm sorry I wasn't in touch. Soon as the body was found, Warren let me know it was Archie, not him. He didn't want me at the hotel anymore, so I've been staying with him and Basil."

I shook my head. Having had a chance to vent my frustrations, the coffee was calming my nerves some. I turned back to Warren. "Alright, there's one more question I haven't been able to answer. Why's the mob after you for money?"

Warren glanced toward Basil. "Blackmail. Razzi's got some photos. If the studio got wind of them, I'd be in for a fight to keep my job."

I nodded. I understood all too well what he meant, since Daisy and I walked on similar dangerous ground. "We need to find Daisy. That's all I'm worried about right now." I looked at Clarisse. "Case solved, right?"

"I'll still pay you—"

I cut her off with a flat hand in her direction. Turning my attention back to Warren, I said, "Help me find my girlfriend."

~

Warren promised he'd do everything he could from his location to help me find Daisy. He started by loaning me a car with a shortwave radio installed in the passenger seat, allowing us to communicate as needed.

I started by swinging by our house—maybe Daisy had been in the shower when I'd called—but there was no sign she'd been home. I checked her side of the bed, the laundry hamper, and the dishrack, but everything suggested our house had remained empty all night.

I took the opportunity to change into something more conducive to investigations and grabbed my guitar case, which I tucked into the trunk of Warren's car.

My next stop was Seacrest Studios. The security guard waved my car past without even asking me to stop and sign in. I suspected he recognized Warren's car and had standing orders to let it pass, since I thought it unlikely Warren would have risked blowing the cover of his alleged demise to call ahead.

Percy waved when he saw me. "That's an odd car to see you getting out of," he murmured when I approached him as he brushed dry lips against both of my cheeks.

"And that's a different suit than the last one I saw you in," I quipped back. "Is Daisy here?"

"No, but her call isn't until four today." He frowned. "What's going on, Sarah?"

I glanced around to make sure no one was near enough to overhear our conversation. "How much has General Justice told you about the assassin in the city?"

"Only that there is one," Percy replied, matching the volume of his voice to mine. "And, well, that our mutual friend is doing much better than his dearly departed brother."

I nodded. Percy knew more than he had let on in our initial conversation, so I had to assume Richard and Warren had brought him up to speed on the who's who of Las Capas' superhero scene, and I needn't be coy with him. "Have you heard of the Factory?"

"Yes, of course."

"The Greek?"

"That does put together the last piece I wasn't certain about," Percy said, his brow furrowing. "Do you think he's gotten Daisy?"

"I don't know. He attacked me at Gloria Graves' event last night, and I haven't been able to find or get ahold of Daisy since. Our mutual friend and his partner extricated me, but Daisy wasn't nearby at the time, and they didn't know she was there."

Percy tilted his head toward Warren's car. "That's the one with the shortwave, yes?"

I nodded.

"If I see her, I'll call our friend and have him inform you immediately."

"Thank you, Percy." I gave him a wan smile. "I do hope we can have a conversation at some point when there's not something awful going on."

"I would cherish that immensely, my dear. Good luck, and be careful."

"Always."

I swung by the theatre next. We'd parked the car nearby, but it wasn't in the lot when I drove by. I jotted down the phone number for the towing company, but when I called them from a pay phone, they hadn't towed our car. That at least suggested Daisy might have left on her own. But if she had, why couldn't I find her?

My next stop was a diner where we sometimes had lunch if we both had time. The cook, Barney, knew us both, and he was able to confirm Daisy hadn't been in.

When I returned to the car, I tried out the shortwave radio to call Warren's house. Basil's voice crackled to life. "Any luck?" he asked.

"None. You?"

"Sorry, Sarah, nothing. But we're still working on it."

I nodded, even though he couldn't see that gesture. "I'm going to make one more stop, and then I'm going to head back to my house. Maybe we've just missed each other."

"That sounds wise."

My final stop was the First Precinct. As much as I hated the thought of reporting Daisy Dean missing, I was beginning to think we needed as many feet on the ground as we could get.

I smelled Daisy's perfume before I spotted her, tucked away in a corner of the station reading a book, still dressed in her finery from the previous evening.

"Daisy!"

She looked up, eyes wide, and tossed the book aside to rush into my arms.

We shared an embrace, and then I moved her back so I could look her in the eyes. "What are you doing here?"

"I came here after the smoke ... thing at the theatre," she said. "I didn't know where you'd gone, so it seemed like the safest place."

Jimmy Cooper stepped out of his office. "Sarah, thank God! Where have you been?"

I hesitated, not able to tell Jimmy the truth without an entire house of lies crashing down around my head. "I guess ... I must have gotten a full whiff of that smoke and just wandered off. Woke up in the park near our house and felt like I'd slept off the worst drunk I've ever been." It was a mix of lies and exaggerations, and I hated doing it, but I needed to keep Warren's secret safe.

"Should we get you checked out?" Daisy asked, her eyes full of concern.

"No, I'm fine now. I've just been worried sick trying to find you. But it's alright now." I turned to Jimmy. "Any news on what the smoke was from?"

"It was a knockout gas, from a little capsule." He indicated the small size with a finger and thumb. "German design, we think. But we don't know where it came from. No likely suspects anywhere near the event last night."

"The Greek has German ties," I murmured. "Just a possible lead."

Jimmy nodded solemnly. "Thanks. I shouldn't keep you. I imagine that ballgown isn't too comfortable, Miss Dean."

"Oh, it's not," Daisy said. "Thank you, Detective Cooper."

Daisy and I walked out of the police station arm in arm.

As soon as we were outside, she murmured, "What's really going on, darling? Your hair does not look like you slept in a park, and you've changed your clothes."

"It's a lot more complicated than that," I said, "and I will explain it all to you as soon as we're home. I just need to make a quick call." Unlocking the passenger side door on Warren's car, I picked up the radio handset.

"Wait, this car looks familiar," Daisy said.

"It's a mutual friend's." I depressed the button to talk on the radio, cutting off any more questions Daisy might have had. "Found her. I'll be in touch soon." I turned it off before anyone could respond. Turning back to Daisy, I said, "I need to return this car later, though, so why don't you follow me home?"

"Alright, Sarah." Daisy's brow furrowed as her gaze swept the borrowed vehicle. "I'll follow you."

CHAPTER FOURTEEN

As I pulled away from the station in Warren's car, Daisy fell in behind me in our car. But in the rearview mirror, I noticed a third car joining our procession—a dark sedan, quite similar to the ones the Fontanellis had been driving when they showed up at Warren Glenn's house.

I couldn't get a good glimpse of the driver, with the distance between our cars, but I could at least tell whoever was in the car was alone. I didn't discount the possibility of other passengers hiding in the backseat, but I thought that seemed less likely.

I was certain Daisy would continue to follow me even if I took a circuitous route home. If the other car did so as well, I'd be certain they were following us. Without indicating my turn, I took a sharp right.

A moment later, Daisy took the same turn. I didn't need to see her face to know she'd be staring at the back end of this strange car I was driving, lips pressed together, puzzling over why I was taking this route.

Another moment passed, and the other car followed.

I sifted through potential routes to our house I might be able to use to lose this pursuer. The freeway was the best option, even if it would annoy Daisy to go out of our way like that. My hope was it might also discourage whoever this was who was following us.

I signaled to enter the on ramp and saw the flash of Daisy's signal behind me. As I accelerated to reach freeway speeds, I saw our pursuer joining us on the on ramp.

It was still early afternoon, so the traffic was thin, not yet supplemented by the later afternoon rush of cars heading home after work. While it meant it was easy to zip down the freeway, it also meant nothing prevented our pursuer from continuing to follow us. I maneuvered between the lanes, Daisy close behind me, but every shift I made was echoed by the third car.

I considered my options, weighing the difficulty of making a sudden exit with the roads beyond each one. Finally, I decided on one of the exits near the marina—it led to a winding road with a few hidden turn-offs. If Daisy could maintain a high level of attention to what I was doing, we might be able to lose our tail.

I flipped the turn signal on for just an instant, hoping Daisy would see it but not turn hers on in response. I watched her signals closely, then glanced at her face in the rearview mirror. Her gaze darted toward the exit I had in mind. Perfect.

At the last possible moment, she and I both merged into the exit lane and took the exit. The third car followed.

I left the exit ramp at a higher than advisable speed, with Daisy right behind me. As the road wound to the right, I scanned for the first turnoff and jerked the steering wheel to leave the main road. Dust plumed around Warren's car as the tires hit the gravel, but I made the turn and sped down the straightaway that led toward an isolated home. Daisy followed me, and I kept moving until we passed a copse of trees that would block view of the cars from the main road. Throwing Warren's car into park, I turned to watch the road behind us.

The third car sped past the turnoff, seemingly not noticing the heavy gravel dust that obscured a portion of the road.

Daisy parked our car behind me and got out, hurrying over to my window. "Sarah, what on earth is going on?" she gasped.

"We were being followed from the precinct. Just lost them."

She let out a long sigh. "Any idea who it was?"

I shook my head. "It looked like a single person, but I couldn't identify them." I paused, pressing my lips together. "I don't think we should go back to the house."

"Why not?"

"Because I've got a few suspicions on who might have been following us. If I'm right, they'll know where we live, and now that they've lost us, they'll head there. So we need to go somewhere else."

"Like where?"

I sighed. "I've got a place in mind, and I'll explain why we're going there after we get there. It's ... complicated."

"It often is with you, darling." Daisy chuckled. "But I'll follow you there."

~

After we parked the cars in the broad circle outside of Warren Glenn's house, Daisy was again at my window before I'd had a chance to exit the car.

"Sarah, darling, do you know whose house this is?"

"I do."

"And his car, too?"

"Yes. He loaned it to me."

Daisy smiled. "So you've cracked the case, right?"

"Yes and no. I've put all of the pieces together, but The Greek is still at large, and we need to find him and stop him so we can also get Gloria Graves." I paused. "There's more, too, but it's not my story to tell. For now, we're all in a bit of danger."

"Yes, we are in danger," Warren said, striding out of the front door. He smiled at Daisy when he reached us. "Good afternoon, Miss Dean. Sorry to have run out in the middle of production and all that." He returned his attention to me. "What are you doing here?"

"Returning your car, for one. Daisy and I were followed. We lost our tail, but I'm guessing our house isn't safe right now."

"And mine is?"

"Relatively, yes." I popped the trunk and removed my guitar case.

"Sarah?" Daisy asked softly.

"It's okay. Warren knows."

"He ... what? Why?" she asked.

I looked at Warren. "This part's up to you."

He shrugged. "Because Sarah and I have worked together in the past. As peers." He paused, to heighten the drama. "I'm Invincible Man."

Daisy's eyes widened, but then a grin spread across her lips. "Oh my gosh, I can't believe it. Here I've been, acting on a film set with Las Capas' biggest superhero?" Then she glanced at me. "No offense, darling."

"None taken," I said. "We'll be safe here, with Sure Shot and Invincible Man here to protect the rest of you."

"Sure Shot?" Warren asked. "Is that ... oh, instead of Huntsman?"

"That's right. What do you think?"

Warren glanced at Daisy, who was beaming at me. "I think that's a good one," he said. "However, I still think this is a rubbish idea, Sarah. This is not a safehouse."

"Would you rather try to make a stand somewhere else?"

Warren's shoulders slumped. "I'd just prefer if Clarisse and Basil, and Miss Dean here, weren't in harm's way."

"They can wait it out in the wine cellar." I paused. "I'm assuming you have a wine cellar in a place this large."

"Yes, of course. I just worry about collateral damage."

"We can ask General Justice to maintain a perimeter—"

Warren shook his head. "The General's not available. Ciclón either. They're dealing with a big crash on the freeway over in Las Cruces."

I hadn't expected we'd be reduced to just Invincible Man and myself to defend the house. But The Greek didn't have powers, at least, just extensive training. "What about Polonium?"

"Maybe, if I can reach him. If he was at the studio, then he may be stuck in traffic."

"Rashimi can fly, so the traffic wouldn't impact her."

With a nod, Warren gestured toward the entryway to his house. "Let's take this discussion inside and give her a call. The neighbors may not be nearby, but I feel a bit exposed, don't you?"

The sun was starting to set, lengthening the shadows of the palm trees around Warren's yard. I nodded and followed him and Daisy inside the house.

"I'll get the others settled. See if Rashimi can help out, and then meet us downstairs."

I dialed Rashimi's number from memory—I didn't need it often, but her number had enough of a pattern to it that it was easy to recall. The phone rang three times before someone picked up.

"Hello?" The voice was husky and heavily accented.

"Is Rashimi in?" I asked. Though it was her superhero identity, it was also her given first name. Being non-Western meant most people assumed it was a pseudonym.

"Yes, she is in, but she cannot come to the phone."

"I'm sorry, I don't want to pry, but this is somewhat urgent. Is there a better time to call back?"

"She prays. One hour before and one hour after sunset."

I didn't think the person on the phone referred to religious prayer, but perhaps a magical meditation of some sort. Either way, I wasn't going to press it. "Thank you. I'll try back later, then."

~

Unsurprisingly, Warren had more than just a wine cellar in the basement of his estate. An entire section was walled off, free of windows, and with comfortable furnishings and tasteful décor. It had its own bathroom and kitchen, almost like a small, secure apartment within the larger house.

"Rashimi isn't available either," I told Warren as I looked around the space. "You don't think they'll be safe here?"

"Collateral damage," he murmured. "The walls are good, but the ceiling here is the floor upstairs. It's not as reinforced as I'd like it."

"Then all we need to do is make sure The Greek doesn't set foot in the house. I can hit him from one of the upper floor balconies. I've got knockout arrows."

"Great. But how do we find him?"

"We'll need to keep a watch out." I glanced back at the rest of our group—the civilians, as I found myself beginning to consider them. "Does Basil, or your sister, do they do anything of note?"

"They can both use a gun. Or at least they've been trained. I don't know that Clarisse is in a good state to have a weapon in hand at the moment."

"Daisy can use a gun as well, but mostly as a way of clearing herself some space." I grinned, thinking about her adorable habit of closing her eyes before she fired. But that wasn't a useful skill in this situation. "Let's just make sure there's a weapon or two available to them? Just in case?"

Warren nodded. "There's a safe. Basil knows the combination."

"Then let's go upstairs and figure out the best vantage points to keep a look out on as much of the estate as we can."

We made it halfway up the stairs before the lights winked out.

"Well, shit," Warren said.

CHAPTER FIFTEEN

The stairway wasn't half as dark as I expected it to be, and I looked around for the source. Luminescence surrounded Warren Glenn. "I never realized glowing was one of your powers."

He looked down at his hands. "Oh, yeah, that. It's not that helpful. It's only visible in darkness, but I glow all the time if I don't concentrate on turning it down."

"It's useful for the moment. Does your house have backup power?"

"The safe room does. The rest of the house is on the public grid. Less suspicious when the neighborhood power goes out."

We reached the first level of the house. It was twilight outside, but the dim light barely made a dent in the darkness of the interior. I couldn't see any of the neighboring houses or streetlights either. "That's a conveniently timed power outage."

"I don't think it's a coincidence."

"Neither do I," I said. "Tamp down your glow."

He did, making it even more difficult to see anything. "Alright, there's a garret on the third floor. That's the best vantage point. It's best for you to go up there. And there's a sunroom that overlooks the bay and the back side of the property. I'll take that position."

"Is there a way to communicate between the two?" I asked.

"Not really. This wasn't set up as a two-man watch job." He paused for a minute. "Do you know Morse code?"

I chuckled. "Yes, of course."

"There's a small dumbwaiter between the garret and the sunroom. If we open both the doors, we can tap out messages. Simple things. S-O-S if you need help."

"H-E-R-E for his arrival?"

Warren nodded. "And once we've spotted him, one of us can move to the other location." We stopped on the second-floor landing, and he gestured at a narrow staircase. "Your garret awaits, milady. I'll be over here."

I set the guitar case down out of the way and removed my bow and arrows. "I'll signal when I'm in position."

He nodded again and moved through the doorway he had indicated, and I ascended the stairs.

The garret was small and cozy, with a lingering scent of tea and ink. A writing desk sat to one side of the room, overlooking the grounds through floor to ceiling windows. I examined the windows and found the crank mechanism that allowed each pane to fold like a small hand fan and be moved out of the way. The breeze brought with it the scent of night-flowering bushes and the faintest hint of the bay, fishy and salty. My nostrils flared, seeking out any other scents. If I caught a whiff of The Greek's tobacco, I knew I'd recognize it.

Reevaluating the garret from an offensive standpoint, I moved the chair away from the writing desk and tucked a standing lamp a little farther behind the armchair that took up a quarter of the room. If The Greek approached from the south, I'd have a difficult time getting a good shot on him, but the east portion of the lawn would be much easier to hit. The north side of the house sat near enough the hillside that it was unlikely anyone would come from that direction. And Warren would have the west and a portion of the south covered, if this garret and the sunroom faced opposite directions.

I opened the dumbwaiter door and tapped out "I-P." In position.

Warren responded with "C-F-M." Confirm.

I scanned the grounds outside the house. Twilight had slipped away on this side, though I imagined Warren still had a few more minutes in the sunroom before it would be completely dark. I hoped he'd remember to keep himself from glowing, or at least remain out of sight of the windows. The Greek's specialty was demolitions, not weaponry, but I didn't doubt he had a good enough throwing arm to launch a grenade or one of those German capsules through a second-floor window. I suspected he might even be able to hit me, up here on the third floor.

Thus far, though, all I could see was faint shadows moving in the breeze. My eyes adjusted to the darkness, and I could pick out the various bushes and trees, but no animals or people moving around in their midst. I set myself up to sweep my line of sight, back and forth, timing even my blinking and my breathing so as to miss as little as possible.

This was my training, long ago as it had been. It was one of the things I excelled at, far above my brother. He could shoot well enough, but he was horrible at waiting. I had the keen eye and the patience. And yet my gender had led my father to declare Matthew as his heir over me.

Ah well, had I stayed in Cobalt City, I wouldn't be here with Daisy, both of us living a life we enjoyed. A life I was going to do everything in my power to maintain.

~

I heard Warren's footsteps on the stairs behind me half an hour after we'd split up. Apparently, the lack of patience was a male superhero trait. I held up my gloved fist, the sign I'd learned in Europe to wordlessly command a stop.

"I don't think this is going to work, Sarah," Warren whispered. "I think we might need to draw him out."

I frowned. "That's a horrible plan. Making yourself a target?"

"I'm the one he's looking for. I can force a confrontation."

"He uses explosives. If you show yourself, what's to stop him from blowing you to smithereens on your front lawn."

"Why do people always forget I'm invincible?" Warren asked.

I started to ask him about how much testing he'd done on his invincibility, but I stopped myself. "Alright, if you think that will protect you, then go ahead. I haven't got a better idea if we want to press this conflict unless I get my detonation arrows and start blowing up parts of your landscaping. Just remember I said it was a bad plan?"

"Noted," he said. "Shoot for a knockout. Try not to blow anything up."

"Of course," I said, tapping my quiver. "I left the detonation arrows downstairs."

I continued scanning the yard as Warren went to stand on his front lawn, glowing again. If I'd been an assassin out to take down an invincible superhero, I wouldn't have allowed him to draw me out like that. Everything about this screamed trap.

But I caught the faintest whiff of tobacco, and I zeroed in on the location where I thought it was coming from. A faint red glow, small, and illuminating nothing more than a point, shone just enough for me to target it. I lowered the tip of my arrow just a hair and fired.

A grunt sounded as the arrow struck home, and I quickly nocked a flare arrow and shot it about a foot left of my previous shot, followed by a second flare arrow about a foot right of the first shot. As they hit ground and illuminated the area, I watched The Greek fall between the pair of flares.

Warren was on the move before I left the garret, and I hurried down the stairs and out the front door to join him. By the time I arrived, he had The Greek bound to a palm tree.

The Greek chuckled when he saw me. Despite being tied to a tree, he still looked polished and suave, his dark hair still neatly in place. "Should have known it was you, Huntsman."

"It's Sure Shot now," I said.

"Noted."

"You knew it was me, and yet you kept coming after my friend here?" I asked. "Shame on you."

He shrugged. "It's a job. Just trying to finish it."

"Are you willing to testify on it?" I asked.

The Greek arched an eyebrow. "In exchange for—"

"You've killed two men," Warren said. "You'll be lucky to not be executed after your imminent conviction."

The Greek regarded Warren. "If it helps, I am sorry I killed your brother."

"It really doesn't, knowing you'd have rather killed me." Warren looked at me. "Clarie hired you for this case. I'm going to go call the police, if you don't mind."

"Ask for Detective Cooper at the First Precinct. I trust him."

Warren nodded and stalked off.

I turned back to The Greek. "Will you testify against the woman who hired you?"

"I suppose you want to hear it all first?" The Greek said with a sigh.

I smiled. "Indulge me."

"Gloria Graves, though I suspect you already knew that name. She's been around for a long time. Longer than you think. She won't be easy to catch. In fact, if word gets to her that I've been arrested, she'll get out of town quick as a wink."

I nodded. She would try to get away, but I hoped we could still get the drop on her. At any rate, I wasn't going to let The Greek see any worry in my expression or poise. "We'll be able to collect her as well, don't worry. Why did she want Warren dead?"

"It was the driver. Warren was just theoretical collateral damage. The driver worked for her a long time ago. When one of the paparazzi got a shot of him leaving a nightclub with Warren, here in Las Capas, she realized her secret was in danger."

"And Angelo Fontanelli?"

"Loose cannon who was figuring out what was going on. Miss Graves had some of the Fontanellis working for her too, but she wanted an outsider to take care of the problem."

I crossed my arms over my chest. "Did you ever consider the possibility she'd want you out of the picture when all was said and done?"

The Greek shrugged as much as he could within his bindings. "She can buy my silence for a pittance compared to these other fools."

"And yet you've just spilled the beans to me."

"Well, you and your friend have me a little tied up at the moment."

I shook my head. I didn't like how neatly all this was falling into place. I'd figured everything out. Everything except the plan to stop Gloria Graves from fleeing once I was sure she was our culprit. "Warren?" I shouted back toward the house.

A moment later, he called back. "What?"

"Call the General, see if he or Ciclón is free to nab Miss Graves before she flees."

The Greek was chuckling again, and my shoulders slumped. I knew it was too easy. "She's gone already, isn't she?" I asked.

"In the wind. We knew it was getting too hot."

"I wouldn't count on her being out of our reach," I said. "Especially not after I talk to Papa Razzi. I suspect he may be interested in restitution for Angelo Fontanelli's death."

"Razzi won't pursue her. She'll pay him off if he tries. Plus, she's got centuries of experience with becoming someone new when the stakes get too high. Face it, Sure Shot. You missed this one."

"You're awfully smug for a man who's about to go away for a long time."

"Am I, though? If I deny every connection I have to Miss Graves, it'll be your word against mine. The cops don't have any reason to want to prove anything beyond that I'm a murderer, and I'll give them that much. And then my high-priced attorney will swing me a deal for a lower security facility, and you know that won't hold me for long."

"You're damned lucky the reformulated truth serum General Justice is working on is going through proper channels, or you'd be singing like a canary on the stand." I shook my head, now just as frustrated with The Greek as Warren had been before the assassin even started talking. "I hope they lock you in a hole and throw away the key."

CHAPTER SIXTEEN

I didn't know why Warren insisted Daisy and I needed to be at his press conference the next day. All I knew was he planned to reassure the world he was alive and also to explain why. He'd promised he wouldn't out me as Sure Shot or the former Huntsman, so I'd agreed to tag along.

Basil and Clarisse waved us down as soon as we arrived. They'd both recovered from being locked into Warren's safe room while we dealt with The Greek, as had Daisy. The three of them had bonded during that time, it seemed, as they all exchanged hugs and kisses on the cheeks.

Clarisse squeezed my hand warmly and presented me with a check.

I squinted at the amount. "This is higher than our agreed upon fee."

"You deserve it," she said.

"Damn right you do," Daisy said, taking the check from me, folding it, and tucking it into my purse.

Basil hugged me with the same fervor he had hugged Daisy. "Thank you, Sarah. You're the reason we're here right now."

I felt like he was giving me a little more credit than I was due, but I didn't want to disabuse him of the notion. I hadn't been thrilled with the way things with The Greek had panned out, and I'd be keeping tabs on his trial and subsequent imprisonment, so I would know the moment he was back on the streets. For the time being, though, getting a bonus on my check and lauded as a hero privately were nice feelings.

"Did anything come of looking for Miss Graves?" Clarisse asked.

I shook my head. "Her house in Rosita Heights was completely empty when Ciclón got there, as though no one had lived there for months. Detective Cooper has some of the Las Capas Police Department keeping an eye on the roads in and out of town, but it's likely too late to catch her."

"She'll get what's coming to her sooner or later, I'm sure," Clarisse said.

I didn't entirely share her optimism, but I hoped I'd get a chance to stop Gloria Graves, Vera Lancaster, or whatever other pseudonym she might choose someday.

Warren took up his position in front of the cameras, smiling and waving as reporters began shouting questions at him. "Let me make my statement first, and then we'll have time for questions," he said, flashing his best movie star smile. He unfolded a piece of paper, but after a quick glance at it, he seemed to be speaking from memory. "On the evening of April twentieth, my boat, *The Invincible*, was destroyed in Las Capas Bay. My brother, Archibald, was on that boat and lost his life in the explosion. But I suspected then and know now that myself and my friend Basil were the real targets of that explosion, so we went into hiding. Thanks to the help of my sister, Clarisse, and her brilliance in choosing Miss Sarah Castile to investigate the explosion and Archie's seeming disappearance, Miss Castile got to the bottom of the case and helped apprehend the culprit through her thorough investigation."

"Oh, bloody hell," Daisy muttered under her breath, her gloved hand covering her mouth.

"What?" I asked. So far, Warren had kept his promise.

"You're about to be the busiest PI in Las Capas, darling."

Half a dozen of the photographers and reporters had turned in my direction when Warren gestured my way. I could only imagine how many of them had already gotten photos of me and Daisy. I was thankful she'd thought to whisper behind her hand.

One of the reporters' questions cut through my thoughts. "How did you and Miss Castile apprehend the culprit, exactly?"

Warren glanced at me and smiled. "Miss Castile was generous enough to offer to play the damsel in distress to draw out the assassin. As for me, there's a secret I've been hiding from my fans for years." He paused dramatically, the way only someone of his caliber could. "I'm Invincible Man."

Well, he'd done it. He'd deflected any potential interest away from me by flipping our roles in apprehending The Greek. It played perfectly for the media. They erupted with questions.

I turned and walked away.

Daisy followed me. "Are you alright, Sarah?"

"He kept his promise," I said. "I don't like being relegated to the damsel in distress, but at least he made it somewhat clear I wasn't *actually* in distress. Just a decoy." I sighed. "It fits the narrative people want to hear, even if it is a lie."

Daisy took my hand and squeezed it softly. "Warren, Basil, and Clarisse will always know the truth, as will you and I. And when it comes down to it, that's what matters, right?"

I squeezed her hand back in response.

~

Catherine didn't normally call me on the weekends, so I was surprised to hear her voice on Saturday afternoon. "Your office line has been ringing non-stop since the story hit the papers this morning. I'm going to drop all of the messages by your office Monday morning, if that's all right. Otherwise, we'll be on the phone for hours while I give you the details."

"Thanks, Catherine. How many—?"

"Oh, a dozen so far, and I don't want to be away from your line for too long. They just keep coming in!"

My mind reeled. A dozen new cases, all based on what Warren had said about me? And more to come? Daisy hadn't been wrong about my newfound celebrity. "Thanks, Catherine. I'm sorry they're all bothering you on a Saturday."

"No bother, Sarah. I'll keep track of what you owe me for the overtime. I think you're good for it."

"Of course. Say, I don't suppose I could entice you to a full-time secretarial role for me, if this keeps up?"

"You send me over a job description and salary offer, and I'll think about it. I can point you to some other girls if I can't take it, of course."

"You're the best, Catherine. Thank you so much."

"Not every day you get to answer calls for the best female PI in Las Capas." A phone rang somewhere in the distance. "Oh, that's your line. Gotta go!"

I looked at Daisy, who leaned in the doorway nearby. "Busy, like I said?"

"A dozen cases waiting for me on my desk on Monday. At least."

"Still make time to come home and eat my cooking?"

"Always," I said, wrapping my arms around her waist to kiss her.

ACKNOWLEDGEMENTS

This is the sort of book that really takes a village. Being part of a shared universe sandbox means that all the other authors writing in that sandbox get a bit of credit, even if I am the sort of kid who goes off into my own corner of the sandbox, builds a fort, and plays alone. But without Nathan Crowder, Jeremy Zimmerman, Erik Scott de Bie, Rosemary Jones, and Amanda Cherry, I wouldn't have a sandbox in which to stake out my corner.

There are also the writers of the writers' group that adopted me who haven't dipped their toes into the sandbox yet, but we'll lure them in sooner or later—Torrey Podmajersky, Sarah Grant, and Sam Merry. Come on in, the water's lovely!

My immense thanks go out to Amanda Robinson and Cyrano Jones, two of the dearest friends and beta readers a girl could have. Thank you for finding my mistakes, giving me nuggets to make what I've written even better, and bouncing ideas back and forth (including "99 Problems and a Boat Ain't One"). Without you, she'd still be Lady Huntsman. You helped her find her new identity.

And forever thanks and love to Jeremy Zimmerman, for letting me write when I could be watching TV with you, and to my mom, Shirley Vogel, who tells everyone who ever knew me, "Dawn's got a new book out!" Every. Single. Time.

ABOUT THE AUTHOR

Dawn Vogel's academic background is in history, so it's not surprising that much of her fiction is set in earlier times. By day, she edits reports for historians and archaeologists. In her alleged spare time, she runs a craft business, co-runs a small press, and tries to find time for writing. Her steampunk adventure series, *Brass and Glass*, is available from DefCon One Publishing. She is a member of Broad Universe, SFWA, and Codex Writers. She lives in Seattle with her husband, author Jeremy Zimmerman, and their herd of cats.

Visit her at http://historythatneverwas.com.

ABOUT THE ARTIST

Luke Spooner, a.k.a. 'Carrion House,' currently lives and works in the South of England. Having recently graduated from the University of Portsmouth with a first class degree, he is now a full time illustrator for just about any project that piques his interest. Despite regular forays into children's books and fairy tales, his true love lies in anything macabre, melancholy, or dark in nature and essence. He believes that the job of putting someone else's words into a visual form, to accompany and support their text, is a massive responsibility, as well as being something he truly treasures. You can visit his web site at www.carrionhouse.com.

www.ingramcontent.com/pod-product-compliance
Lightning Source LLC
Chambersburg PA
CBHW060937120626
46557CB00003B/1033